D0588844

THE MAN
WHO KILLED
J.D. SALINGER

A LOOKING FOR LOVE STORY

BY THAT BASTARD J.D. CALIFORNIA

Gigolo Publishing
Suite 389, 22 Notting Hill Gate
W11 3JE, London
United Kingdom
www.gigolopublishing.com

Design by Sheer Design and Typesetting

ISBN 9789186283759

FIRST CHAPTER

A man walks into a bar across the street from a brothel. On his right shoulder sits his pet duck, on his left his pet monkey. He nods towards the bartender and says, "Bartender, I'd like an alligator with a twist of lime, please." The bartender takes a good look at both the duck and the monkey, turns to the Irishman on his left, then to the priest on his right, and finally to the dwarf just coming out of the bathroom. Through the window he spots a chicken, a rabbi, and a Lutheran minister about to cross the road.

"Well," the man with the pet duck and the pet monkey says. "What are you waiting for?" and finally the bartender looks the man square in the face and says, "You stupid fuck." The end.

This is my life. One complete and utterly useless compilation of one shitty, incomprehensible joke after another. It doesn't make sense, whichever way you look at it. And worst of all, I'm beginning to suspect there's no bloody punch line.

When I was a kid, I loved jokes. They were the cream on the cake for me, the slap on my bony knee, and I hee-hawed my way through adolescence. But I don't anymore, hee-haw. Perhaps humor comes with a best-before date. Time rolls by, things change, and fewer and fewer things make the cut. Suddenly life's episodes have become shortened versions of themselves—novelettes, or haiku, blurbs that blare out constant presentation of our personas. I am a smiley. I like. I beep. I tweet. I update. A life condensed in two hundred words or less.

Granted, without summaries none of us would exist. Perhaps it's because today we are so many things, compared to fifty years ago. It used to be you were a farmer, or a doctor, or a sailor, but today you can be so much more. An entrepreneur, a blogger, a promoter, a cupcake baker, a life coach, AND run an urban community farm for organic veggies on your rooftop. We are so much more, most of the time, yet we feel less, all of the time. It's the most pronounced irony of the twenty-first century: living in the age of labeling while doing everything you can not to be caught with a label.

Anyway. If I pretended to be someone else, this would be my label:

Meet John David California. He is the single, lonely, and bored gentleman around whom this story revolves. As if being generally confused by life wasn't enough, he also just recently killed one of the world's most famous authors—a true legend, and one of the last great ones. But in John David's defense, he didn't do it on purpose. It just sort of happened. Old age, another one ripe for picking. But regardless of John David's innocence, the death of the famous author sent shock waves through both the literary elite and the lowlier literary masses. It was more than a faux pas. Who would be next, the vibers vibed in unison? Poor old Harper Lee? And all because of a book called *60 Years Later*, which was meant to catapult him into literary acknowledgment at least, and perhaps even stardom and fame. Instead it fell flat and wet, like a turd from a giant seagull.

Consequently, in this misery that Schopenhauer called everyday life, John David drifts along. And like so many others he drifts no place exciting. More often than not, the undiluted stream of shit traverses only the not-so-thrilling distance between his office cubicle and his apartment cubicle.

My ex-girlfriend once said that only narcissists and the insane talk about themselves in third person. I told her that sometimes it's easier to look down at people from a rooftop than to spot the bastard spying on you from above. She went on to say I had issues—she was a psychology major, so I guess she should know. In hindsight I should have told her to stuff it up her muff. It's the straight-backed and faultless ones we should be worried about. The ones who stitch up and hide their foibles so well that there has to be a reason. I wouldn't be surprised if she one day turns out to be a serial killer. Or at least one of those people who collect their poop in glass jars. But I mustn't talk about my ex-girlfriend. Memories are nails in my Jesus wrists. Instead, let me tell you about my cubicle.

This is my cubicle. Granted, it's really more of a rectangular prism than a cubicle, but that's how most things seem to be these days. Nothing matches up to its description. Cubicles are rectangular prisms, and limousines are puke-smelling cabs. Everything is made up to be grander than it really is. I'm not sure when it happened or who's at fault. But, there's no denying reality. Words have deflated in value. Nothing means what it used to.

So for once, in the name of truth, let's call things what they really are. This is my rectangular prism. My rectangular prism is where I spend half of my waking hours. That's the reason I have plastered it with posters. Actually, with the decline of words in mind, I'd have to say that "plastered" is an overstatement. The truth is that my walls only hold two posters and a bunch of Post-it notes.

The first poster is one of Tom Hulce playing Wolfgang Amadeus Mozart in the movie *Amadeus*. He's got a great laugh in that movie: loud, shrill, and unapologetic. *Amadeus* won eight Oscars on account of that laugh, and that's why I have the poster. Not because I love the movie, but to remind myself never to underestimate a great cachinnation. One day, ideally, I'd like to choose my woman by her chuckle. I wish for it to be pearly and seductive, like a stalling motor vehicle, and not at all like *Amadeus*. This is the true reason for the poster. To remind me of that one-day woman.

I know it's not proper to bring your dreams to work. It's sort of like hanging *Mona Lisa* on the wall in a kindergarten—the colors look real good, but the value of the painting is hopelessly deflated.

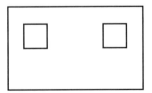

The second poster is the Mona Lisa. I like the irony. Besides, in many ways this place really is like a kindergarten.

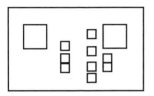

The Post-it notes are all related to my job. There are twenty-eight of them in total, and each one contains an alias. That's right: I am many different persons at work. I'm an official multiple-personality [dis]orderly. Twenty-eight active personas, and God only knows how many inactive are just sitting out there. There must be thousands floating around.

I'll let that sit with you for a wee bit. A gold star to anyone who figures it out. (Hint: It's not a football team.)

What I'd really like is to tell you about Diane, but first I think I'll have to tell you about Bri.

Bri knows me as one of the people in what she calls the creative department. It's another label, the same way we use *correctional facility* instead of the *slammer* and *dental assistant* instead of *human floss*. To me it's simply the Bullshit Department. For obvious reasons I've never let this reach Bri's ears. She'd suffocate on her own saliva.

Bri's a power woman, around forty, and a sparkling version of it. I've never seen her in anything else, so my conclusion is she has built-in high heels. Her yoga-stretched body tiptoes forward when she's not driving around in a sporty convertible. Her polished skin glows unnaturally bright, as if the lasers and tasers have permanently adhered to her and there are rumors of a younger piece of meat waiting at home in the stylish penthouse. She's got the works. She's the American soap-opera dream personified.

Even more pronounced than her skin and her limber, bamboo-pole body is the small, private cloud of efficiency that follows in her wake. It has a thundercloud effect: people get fidgety and fervently try to get out from under it. Even her name is efficient—Bri—so as not to waste any precious time. Nobody knows what it's short for, but we keep a list ("we" meaning me and Diane). Right now it's tied between Brianne and Bridget. My money is on Bridget because she reminds me of Playboy bunny Bridget Marquardt, only with a sharper brain.

Proximity to Bri causes another paranormal occurrence, apart from the fidgeting: around her, you can't help but feel you are a wheel in a greater machine, one that is completely replaceable as long as there are spare parts available. And if there's one thing history—and high school—has taught us, it's that there will always be spare parts available. It's nothing short of amazing how many of us there are, all ready to throw ourselves in front of a bullet. It's obvious Bri cares about one thing only, but I don't hold it against her. It's all about me.

Back to the gold star. Anyone? If I say:

Well, keep your panties on, I won't keep you guessing. It's online dating. How about them apples? Or should I say, how about them lonely souls? Because that's basically what online dating is built around. As the fix is to the junkie, so online dating is to the lonely. It's a ride on the I-Give-a-Fuck-About-You Express. Albeit a short ride, but at least it gives the illusion of movement. And Bri is the commander in chief.

When online dating was just a baby, Bri was matchmaking the old-fashioned way. She interviewed "clients" in person, then used her social network to connect the dots. It was all small-scale, but once she opened her eyes to the information railway it wasn't long until she had created a small online empire. And she rode it mercilessly, hooting and chugging all the way to the bank.

Our manuals (yes, we have manuals, just like the changelings at McDonald's, even though we work nowhere near boiling oil) list several reasons for online dating. It's written from a customer perspective and offers a very general understanding of why the public wants to use our services and how we can help them help themselves, thus helping ourselves and blah blah yakety blah.

Anyway, the manual gives a variety of credible reasons why one would sink so low as to surrender one's hopes to online dating. But no matter what it says, it all comes down to this: people are lonely. Bri's known that for a long time. It's also true that people are lazy, and online dating is like the magic pill that removes both your headache and your constipation—in a flash, but without the splash, if you catch my drift.

Magic pills, now that's something I'll have to take up with Diane.

It's time the two of you met. I haven't, and I mean that. Visually, this is all I know about her.

I call her Diane because that's how she signs off on her messages, but I'm fairly sure it isn't her real name. It all started when they installed an in-house messaging system for the near-instantaneous sharing of information such as profiles, presentation texts, stats, and useful expressions. Officially it's called the Support Fort. "Fort" because it's isolated from the outside…get it?

But Diane and I call it the Support Group, and that's how we got started.

We all have numbers—everyone who works on either of the two floors had a number assigned to them the day they started. On the day of the Support Fort's launch I randomly scrolled though the list of numbers, and just for kicks I nudged number 3—Babe Ruth's number. I'm not sure why, but I wrote something like "Need support. Bottle is near and the end is nigh." Almost instantly I got a reply.

> Hello, my name is Diane and I'm a googleaholic.

Thus began our little soap-opera of flibbertigibbeting. Through the Support Fort we send each other random thoughts and facts, anything we find interesting. Our minds seem to be similarly wired. I send her something about the two Coreys; she sends me something about the Horsehead Nebula. During this diddle-daddling we never ask any personal questions, no how-are-you's, how's-your-day's, or any of those life-fillers. We are connected by what we do and where we are, but that's the extent of it. We haven't talked on the phone, and we haven't exchanged numbers. All we do is trade information. Velcro was invented by George de Mestral when he noticed burrs caught on his dog's legs. Have you heard about the butterflies? And so on. Our relationship is that of two human servers.

However, messaging Diane isn't the only reason I have a cubicle. Even though we, as a company, are chugging forward, all does not move by its pretty self. For one thing, the competition is fierce, and keeping our edge is where my department comes in.

THE BULLSHIT DEPARTMENT

In the Bullshit Department we do what you'd expect us to do. We bullshit. I'm sure this doesn't surprise you all that much. We're all in it up to our necks, constantly regurgitating the bullshit spilled on us daily. Once in a lifetime, each of us has that first moment of realization that the things we thought were genuine and real are really only bullshit. It's part of growing up, becoming an adult. Santa dies a million deaths every year for this very reason.

My contribution to the bullshit stack has even earned me a special title, albeit a self-proclaimed one. Bri would rather swallow a cyanide tablet (and would no doubt live through it) than let it be known. But the expression has spread among the ranks. I'm what we refer to as a faker.

Here's the one-on-one on online dating. You go to any dating site, and what you'll find are a number of products that don't exist.

They seem to exist because people like me put them there, but the pictures are simply images procured in large data files from unscrupulous international corporations specializing in such, and the texts are the creations of hired minds. It's all about getting the edge. It's all about attracting members. It's all about faking.

100 a day $\Longrightarrow$ 35,000 ads/year

I do about one hundred a day, spreading them out over our five sister sites. It doesn't sound like a lot, but in a year my output is approximately 35,000 ads, each of which gets an average of 350 replies, totaling 12,250,000 lonely people. But more important than the millions of replies is the one commandment by which we all abide: *I shall generate new members.* It's the single most important task for anyone, regardless of who you are. You happen to be the girl in the reception, well, shit out of luck, you'd better be generating new members. New members are our crop, and I am one of many digital farmers here to water it.

There are two ways I can do this: fishing and baiting. Obviously these aren't the words used in the manual. (A note for future reference: from here on I'm just skipping the manual completely. That's right, I'm a renegade, a lonesome rider, the sunset hero on his horse called I-Don't-Give-a-Damn.)

When baiting, I simply write profiles that I know will appeal to a certain group of people. These profiles are posted on other online dating sites in order to draw new members to our sites.

When fishing, I use one of my many Post-it note profiles, which are kept alive on our sites to seduce and entice already active members. I contact them and get their hopes up, feeding their dreams. This makes them stick with us. It's the classic junkie-in-the-schoolyard setup. You give them a taste of paradise, and from then on they will be always at your side in the hopes of scoring again.

According to Bri, this is the part of the job we don't talk about. Consequently, it's also the part of the job that is underlined in the confidentiality agreement we all had to sign. Ironically, it is also the only part of the job that I find remotely interesting—being someone else. If only for a little while, and if only in one dimension.

SECOND CHAPTER

I'll have you know that I wasn't always this glum. Believe it or not, I was once quite the happy camper. It's just that life won't leave me alone. It must constantly remind me of the things I don't have. Take yesterday morning, for example.

I get up and discover that my toilet has flooded the bathroom and I have to wait over an hour for the super to arrive. When he finally takes over, I sprint to the subway only to find that there is a technical problem, so I don't make it to work until eleven. And up to here the bad stuff hasn't even started.

It was supposed to get easier. Like how riding your bike was hard at first, but one day you had it, and from there on it was a straight and proud march to bicycling heaven. It's only life that gets harder the longer you do it. But nobody tells you that before you are so wrapped up in it that it's too late.

When I get home from work I see the dirty footprints in the stairwell outside my door. Inside I follow them to the bathroom, where there is a whirlwind of them, as if the plumber and the super celebrated fixing the toilet with a polka. And this is the moment that life hits me. Life, to whom I've been nothing but kind since I was born, give or take a few misplaced scraps of garbage, socks me one right in the kisser. It's about the only thing left of hers, and I cringe when I see it sitting there.

Swedish for *heartbreak*

The bucket is black and has a sticker with a pirate skull on it. There was a time in history when everything from ties to key rings came emblazoned with a Jolly Roger. I'm sure it will baffle archeologists in a century or so, but for me—from that moment on, and throughout my entire life—the Jolly Roger will only represent heartache.

I remember the day we got it. It was a Sunday, and we had borrowed someone's car and crammed it full of things at IKEA. There was literally no room left in the car, and however we tried we just couldn't fit the bucket inside. In the end she had to hold it out the window as I drove, all the way back home.

Everything in that car is gone now, except the bucket and some sort of potato-masher jimmy that I've never used. Every little thing, including her.

I am in a fog as I fill the bucket and mop the floor clean, thinking that it is possible to get anything at IKEA. Almost anything.

Back to work. Work is glorious, a real lifesaver for people like me. Without work we would simply sit alone in our apartments until we disintegrated into piles of dust. Work is what keeps us sane in an otherwise insane world. The only thing we know for certain is that no matter how hard we try, we never seem to successfully match our mental dispositions to the world. There's always a scar shining through somewhere.

I'll tell you a bit more about my job. This is day one, by the way. We are up to date. From here on everything that happens is real-life reality, hi-fi ultrapure resolution, coming to you as it unfolds. Seriously, I'm not joking. The story starts now.

THIRD CHAPTER

If life is what you make of it, then life is a fucking cliché. I should really get paid a lot more for what I do. Risk and damage, just like employees at a nuclear plant. The stuff people pour over me all day, it has to be affecting me in some way. Many times, after periods of diving deep into the ads, I feel sick to my stomach. It's not psychological, it's physical. I feel like regurgitating, and I know exactly where it's coming from. Had this been Chernobyl, it would have been the little green sticks of plutonium, but here the plutonium spells A-V-E-R-A-G-E P-E-O-P-L-E and their empty insides. *I love to eat. I love to laugh. I like to do things for fun. I like going for walks. I like quiet nights in AND fun nights out on the town.* Holy shit, now that really makes a unique and special someone. Looking inside the average person's head is about as exciting as opening a can of baked beans and discovering… that's right, baked beans.

My saving grace is that my job is pretty easy once you get the hang of it. Almost too easy. I spew these profiles out like there's no tomorrow, and I'm not even over 50 percent of my capacity. Let's just say I know how to lay it down in order to catch the fish. I don't know if it's because my capacity is great or because people are so easy to predict. I'd like to flatter myself and think the latter. My job is about knowing what people dream about, what they want, what they fear and desire. My job is being a detective of the soul, a reverse psychologist who creates scenarios rather than analyzing them. I put the pot of gold at the end of the rainbow— the rainbow that in most cases is nothing but a colored cutout on the lens.

Needless to say, given my swift production, there's a lot of leftover time to be put to good use. Diane is my accomplice there, my brotheresse in arms. Today, however, I work for hours before she pops up on the screen. She offers me a piece about how, during the First World War, the juice of young coconuts was used as blood plasma for injured soldiers. I think about this as I author an ad around a female banker who, despite her hectic work schedule and just-terrific friends, has become tired of being alone. I wonder if it would work the other way, nurturing young coconuts with human blood, and I make a note that I must find out.

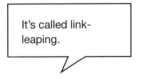

I've got a great idea.

Diane hits me with this right after lunch. My work is pretty much done, meaning I have done what I must to get away with not doing anything else.

It's called link-leaping.

It turns out there is a new game spreading around the Web like wildfire. Not that it surprises me—all sorts of weird things happen online all the time, and as long as we hear that it's the latest craze, we accept it. No matter if it is a game where you recreate the entire cast of your favorite movie by molding figures out of your own shit: if you only add, "it's the new craze on the Web," people will automatically say, "Oh, yes, I think I've heard of it. I've actually been wanting to do *Breakfast at Tiffany's*. In fact, I feel a Holly Golightly coming on right now."

But the game to which Diane wants to draw my attention isn't about decomposed food particles. Link-Leaping is a tad more sophisticated.

Link-Leaping is played on Wikipedia, that giant spittoon of free information. Anyone can put an article on Wikipedia, but nobody can tell with certainty whether it's entirely true or not. The only metric seems to be that if it makes it up there, it's true— sort of like a dog chasing its own tail, or any other proverbial yin-yang that suits.

Basically, Link-Leaping is a game where you follow link after link on Wikipedia until you come back to where you started. Say you choose Mike Tyson as a starting point, and from there you click any of the blue links on the page that strikes your fancy, on and on, until you one day, with a little help from the viral gods, make it back to Mike Tyson's wiki page. Congrats, you've come full wikicircle! You've accomplished nothing.

As far as Diane and I understand it there's no purpose to Link-Leaping, other than getting slightly older. It's just a champion way of passing time. I have to say I've heard better sales pitches, but what have I got to lose, other than the ass-dragging minutes of my life?

We decide to start tomorrow. The rest of the day I spend frantically shuffling ads onto the Web, as if trying to put out a blazing fire of loneliness. At one point Bri dashes through the office—you can actually sense when that happens, just as a shark can sense the slightest disruptions in the water from miles away. We, the employees, office workers of America united, instantly become a flock of starlings. Even though we don't particularly like one another, at times of danger we stick together; it makes it harder for the predator to single out any one of us. Luckily, this time, she passes through without stopping.

I end my shift at exactly 1600 hours, and by 1615 I am on the train home, where life leads me on a detour.

A matter of inconceivable occurrences keeps me from getting off at my station: like a slobbering fool, I follow her, the inconceivable occurrence, complete with a cloud of red hair, all the way to Coney Island. The tomfoolery ends there; I lose her on the platform. In any case, my plan doesn't encompass actual contact, just the stalking bit, and I find myself at the bottom of the steps, right across the street from the amusement park, alone and not at all impressed with myself. On top of it all it's a dirty, gloomy day, the kind only industrialized America could have produced. Seagulls are cruising on cold wafts of air, the general decline of a once booming community showing through every seam. It's like any old Bruce Springsteen song, just take your pick. A song about a once-upon-a-time feeling: pure, but forever lost in history. The block in front of me was meant to be filled with summer crowds and old-fashioned good-time nostalgia, but it manages to give off only a tiny whiff of it. Just enough to make you sad. Perhaps it's the season, the dead leaves, the graying. A ski resort in summer, that's the dread I'm talking about. Misplacement is where it's at, the sadness. Neon in broad daylight.

Back in my apartment I quickly notice that nothing has changed. No earthquake has brought it all down, no fire has scalded the walls, no burst pipe has flooded the floor. Everything is exactly the same. I try to shoo it away, the dullness. I order Chinese, I bomb in front of the TV, but it's too late. The Coney Islandness attached itself to me, and now I have brought it home. It has crept into my sanctuary. My apartment has become that summer ski resort. But then, just when the feeling is at its deepest, to the muted action of yet another *CSI*—city unknown—it hits me. Diane, bless her anonymous soul, must have sensed my desperation. I'm reminded of tomorrow's game, and there it is, my starting point. Like a manifestation of life's mystery: Coney Island. There may be a reason for things that happen after all.

FOURTH CHAPTER

It's a brand-new day, with brand-new possibilities. Anything can happen if I only let life take me where it will. If I only let go. If I only love myself. I have this set of affirmations on my fridge. They are stuck to it with magnets and I change their position every morning, pushing a new one to the top. Nobody knows about them but me, except perhaps for my ex, who put them there in the first place. But she tended toward increasing forgetfulness about everything that was us towards the end. I first called it selective heartache but am now leaning more towards cold-bitch syndrome.

Anyway, if there's one thing it's easy to knock, it's all the freaking new-agers. They seem to come out of every corner, especially here in New York City. As if this was the cosmic pinpoint of the world. I can't help but think that if I was a higher entity, a revelation or an astral force, I'd choose almost any place other than New York City to let my light shine. But hey, that's me.

At the office. I could tell you more about my days here, but that's not going to be very exciting. That would be like you pretending to be me, if only for a little while, while I'm working all day trying my best to be somebody other than myself. It would be too complex a thought pattern to follow, and we would risk disrupting the entire cosmos. So we shan't. Let me save you the time, in case you haven't got it. My days at the office are all the same. I come here, I do the ads, I try to stay away from Bri, all while hating myself for keeping a job that is basically no good for anyone in the world and will lead not to gold, nor to self-realization, nor to anything that will be remembered by anyone within a year from now. If I wanted to talk about my job I would have joined the lunchroom mafia. I only knock out ads to make my life go faster, so I can be an old man sooner rather than later, and then nobody will look down on me when I'm griping about how much my life sucks. The real benefits of a ripe old age. I'm only working so I don't have to realize how much I hate my job. Make sense?

Instead, let's move on to today's main event. (Drumroll and machinegun clatter in perfect unison) That's right, Link-Leaping.

What you got?

This is Diane asking me where I've decided to start. I tell her Coney Island, but for reasons of self-preservation I leave out the reason why.

Coney Island ...

And without further ado, Diane declares the Link-Leaping officially commenced.

CONEY ISLAND

Native American inhabitants, the Lenape, called the island *Narrioch* (land without shadows), because, as is true of other south shore Long Island beaches, its compass orientation keeps the beach area in sunlight all day. The Dutch name for the island was *Conyne Eylandt* meaning *Rabbit Island*. As on other Long Island barrier islands, Coney Island had many and diverse rabbits and rabbit hunting prospered until resort development eliminated their habitat.

Coney Island became a resort after the Civil War as excursion railroads and the Coney Island & Brooklyn Railroad streetcar line reached the area in the 1860s, and the Iron steamboat company in 1881. With the rail lines, steamboat lines and access to the beach came major hotels and public and private beaches, followed by horse racing, amusement parks, and less reputable entertainments such as Three-card Monte, other gambling entrepreneurs, and prostitution.

From 1885 to 1896, the first sight to greet immigrants arriving in New York, even before they saw the Statue of Liberty, was **The Coney Island Elephant.**

THE CONEY ISLAND ELEPHANT

In 1885, the Elephant Hotel, also known as the Elephantine Colossus, was built by James V. Lafferty and was 122 feet high with seven floors and had 31 rooms.

The hotel coined the phrase "going to see the elephant", meaning going to see a prostitute, this because The Coney Island Elephant was really a **brothel** built in the shape of an elephant. In 1896 it burnt down in one of the Island's many fires.

BROTHEL

A brothel, also known as a bordello, cathouse, whorehouse, sporting house, gentleman's club and various other names, is an establishment specifically dedicated to prostitution, providing the prostitutes a place to meet and to have sexual intercourse with clients.

Until recently, in several armies around the world, a mobile brothel service was attached to the army as an auxiliary unit, especially attached to combat units on long-term deployments abroad.

Because it is a touchy subject, military brothels were often designated with creative euphemisms. A notable example of such jargon is "The Candy Box".

In the United States, Nevada is the only state where brothels are legal. Brothels have existed in Nevada since the old mining days of the 1800s and were first licensed in 1971. The legendary **Mustang Ranch** operated from 1971 through 1999.

THE MUSTANG RANCH

The Mustang Ranch, originally known as the Mustang Bridge Ranch, was a brothel in Storey County, Nevada, eight miles east of Reno.

Under owner Joe Conforte, it became Nevada's first licensed brothel in 1971, and soon also the largest with 166 acres (67 ha), and the most profitable.

The prostitutes lived on the ranch during their entire shift, which lasted from several days to several weeks. In the 1970s, the women were bikini clad. Their shifts lasted 12 hours per day and they served six customers on average. Women had to pay for their rooms and for any vendors who came to the Ranch. Medicine and cosmetics were purchased by non-prostitute employees who lived in Sparks, Nevada. Doctors came to the ranch to do pelvic exams and check for sexually transmitted diseases. The only time women were allowed out was during menstruation.

Las Vegas reporter Colin McKinlay visited the Mustang Ranch to do one of the first reports ever allowed by Mustang management. He wrote,

"The women were the most beautiful of any fantasy of man. The line-up contained the most pale of Nordic blonde to the midnight of ebony; a wide eyed waif and wrinkled senior; rail thin to pudgy; tall women stood next to near **dwarfs***, all to answer the buzzer."*

DWARFS

Dwarfism is short stature resulting from a particular medical condition. It is sometimes defined as an adult height of less than 4 feet 10 inches (147 cm), although this definition is problematic because short stature in itself is not a disorder.

Dwarfism can be caused by about 200 distinct medical conditions, such that the symptoms and characteristics of individual people with dwarfism vary greatly. In the United States and Canada, many people with dwarfism prefer to be called little people.

Depiction of dwarfs is also found in European paintings and many illustrations. Many European paintings (especially Spanish) of the 16th–19th centuries depict dwarfs by themselves or with others. In the Talmud, it is said that the second born son of the Egyptian Pharaoh of the Bible was a dwarf. Recent scholarship has suggested that ancient Egyptians held dwarfs in high esteem.

See also

– **Gigantism**

GIGANTISM

Gigantism, also known as giantism (from Greek *gigas*, *gigantas* "giant"), is a condition characterized by excessive growth and height significantly above average. This condition is caused by an over production of human growth hormone. The professional wrestler **Andre the Giant** is the most famous person to possess this condition.

ANDRE THE GIANT

André René Roussimoff (19 May 1946 – 27 January 1993), best known as André the Giant, was a French professional wrestler and actor. He is recognized from his role as Fezzik in the classic movie *The Princess Bride*. His great size was a result of gigantism, and led to him being dubbed "The Eighth Wonder of the World".

André was discovered by Lord Alfred Hayes, a wrestling promoter, and left home as a teenager to become a wrestler in Paris. He worked as a mover by day and trained in the ring at night – though few wrestlers were willing to train with anyone so large and strong. In 1964, Édouard Carpentier, a well-known French wrestler, agreed to train with him. Roussimoff was billed as "Géant Ferré", the name of a legendary French lumberjack, and quickly made a name for himself. For the next few years, he wrestled in arenas and carnivals in Europe, New Zealand, and Africa.

After wrestling in Japan, Roussimoff followed Carpentier to Montreal, Canada, where he was an immediate success. He decided to change his name to "André the Giant".

André was one of WWF's most beloved "babyfaces" throughout the 1970s and early 1980s and he was mentioned in the 1974 Guinness Book of World Records as the highest paid wrestler in history up to that time. He had earned $400,000 in one year alone during the early 1970s.

In the A&E documentary, *Biography*, Arnold Skaaland mentions how André wished he could see a Broadway play. Arnold offered to buy tickets, but André then passed up the opportunity, citing how he was too big for the seats and that people behind him would not be able to see. This was cited as a principal reason for why André frequented taverns more than anywhere else.

André has also been unofficially crowned "The Greatest Drunk on Earth" for once consuming 119 12-ounce beers in 6 hours. On an episode of WWE's *Legends of Wrestling*, Mike Graham claimed that André once drank 197 16-ounce beers in one sitting, which was confirmed by Dusty Rhodes. Such feats can be attributed to his much larger than usual size, meaning it would take higher volumes of liquor to inebriate him. In her autobiography, The Fabulous Moolah alleges that André drank 327 beers and passed out in a hotel bar in **Reading**, Pennsylvania, and because the staff could not move him, they had to leave him there until he regained consciousness.

READING

Reading is a city in southeastern Pennsylvania, USA, and seat of Berks County. Overlooking the city on Mount Penn is Reading's symbol, a Japanese-style pagoda visible from everywhere in town and referred to locally as "the Pagoda".

The city lent its name to the now-defunct Reading Railroad, which brought anthracite coal from the Pennsylvania Coal Region to cities along the Schuylkill River. The railroad is one of the four railroad properties in the classic United States version of the Monopoly board game.

During the general decline of heavy manufacturing, Reading was one of the first localities where outlet shopping became a tourist industry. It has been known as "The Pretzel City" because of numerous local **pretzel** bakeries.

PRETZEL

A pretzel is a type of baked food made from dough in soft and hard varieties and savory or sweet flavors in a unique knot-like shape, originating in Europe.

Schloss Burg is renowned for a 200-year-old specialty, the "Burger pretzel". A local story says that the recipe came from a grateful Napoleonic soldier in 1795, whose wounds were treated by a baker's family in the little town of Burg. The cultural importance of the pretzel for Burg is expressed by a monument in honor of the pretzel bakers, and by an 18-km hiking trail nearby called "Pretzel Hiking Trail".

The annual United States pretzel industry is worth over $550 million. The average American consumes about 1.5 pounds (0.7 kg) of pretzels each year.

The privately run "Pretzel Museum" opened in Philadelphia in 1993.

In Fashion: The sling **bikini** pretzel bathing suit design emerged in the early 1990s, as a new fashion product of Spandex.

BIKINI

Bikini Atoll (also known as Pikinni Atoll) is a World Heritage listed atoll in the Micronesian Islands of the Pacific Ocean, part of Republic of the Marshall Islands.

The atoll has always been called Bikini by the native Marshall Islanders, from Marshallese "*Pik*" meaning "surface" and "*Ni*" meaning "coconut". The name was popularized in the United States because the bikini swimsuit was named after the island in 1946.

As part of the Pacific Proving Grounds it was the site of more than 20 nuclear weapons tests between 1946 and 1958. The two-piece swimsuit was introduced within days of the first nuclear test on the atoll, when the name of the island was in the news. Introduced just weeks after the one-piece "Atome" was widely advertised as the "smallest bathing suit in the world", it was said that the bikini "split the atome".

Through its history, the atoll symbolizes the dawn of the **nuclear age**, despite its paradoxical image of peace and of earthly paradise.

NUCLEAR AGE

The Atomic Age, also known as the Nuclear age, is a phrase typically used to delineate the period of history following the detonation of the first nuclear bomb Trinity on July 16, 1945.

The phrase "Atomic Age" was coined by William L. Laurence, a New York Times journalist who became the official journalist for the U.S. **Manhattan Project** which developed the first nuclear weapons.

THE MANHATTAN PROJECT

The Manhattan Project was the codename for a project conducted during World War II to develop the first atomic bomb, before Germany or Japan.

The Manhattan Project, which began as a small research program in 1939, eventually employed more than 130,000 people and cost nearly US$2 billion ($22 billion in present day value). The project's roots began when a letter was sent to President Franklin D. Roosevelt, expressing concerns that Nazi Germany might develop nuclear weapons. The letter was signed by **Albert Einstein**.

ALBERT EINSTEIN

Albert Einstein (14 March 1879 – 18 April 1955) was a theoretical physicist, philosopher and author who is widely regarded as one of the most influential and iconic scientists and intellectuals of all time.

In 1916, he published a paper on the general theory of relativity. In 1917, Einstein applied the general theory of relativity to model the structure of the universe as a whole.

On the eve of World War II in 1939, he personally alerted President Franklin D. Roosevelt that Germany might be developing an atomic weapon, and recommended that the U.S. begin uranium procurement and nuclear research. Days before his death, however, Einstein signed the Russell–Einstein Manifesto, that highlighted the dangers posed by the military usage of nuclear energy.

In 1922, Einstein traveled throughout Asia and later to Palestine, as part of a six-month excursion and speaking tour. His travels included Singapore, Ceylon, and Japan, where he gave a series of lectures to thousands of Japanese. His first lecture in Tokyo lasted four hours, after which he met the emperor and empress at the Imperial Palace where thousands came to watch. Einstein later gave his impressions of the Japanese in a letter to his sons: "Of all the people I have met, I like the Japanese most, as they are modest, intelligent, considerate, and have a feel for art."

On April 17, 1955, Albert Einstein experienced internal bleeding caused by the rupture of an abdominal aortic aneurysm, which had previously been reinforced surgically by Dr. Rudolph Nissen in 1948. Einstein refused surgery, saying: "I want to go when I want. It is tasteless to prolong life artificially. I have done my share, it is time to go. I will do it elegantly." He died in Princeton Hospital early the next morning at the age of 76, having continued to work until near the end.

Einstein's remains were cremated and his ashes were scattered around the grounds of the Institute for Advanced Study.

During the autopsy, the pathologist of Princeton Hospital, Thomas Stoltz Harvey, removed Einstein's brain for preservation, without the permission of his family, in hope that the neuroscience of the future would be able to discover what made Einstein so intelligent.

Einstein received the 1921 Nobel Prize in Physics. He published more than 300 scientific along with over 150 non-scientific works, and received honorary doctorate degrees in science, medicine and philosophy from many European and American universities; he also wrote about various philosophical and political subjects such as socialism, international relations and the **existence of God.**

EXISTENCE OF GOD

In philosophical terminology, arguments for and against the existence of God involve primarily the sub-disciplines of epistemology (theory of knowledge) and ontology (nature of being), but also of the theory of value, since concepts of perfection are so often bound up with notions of God.

One problem posed by the question of the existence of God is that traditional beliefs usually ascribe to God various supernatural powers. Other arguments against the existence of God are:

1. The argument from inconsistent revelations contests the existence of the deity called God as described in scriptures by identifying apparent contradictions between different scriptures.

2. The problem of evil contests the existence of a god who is both omnipotent and omnibenevolent by arguing that such a god should not permit the existence of evil or suffering.

3. The destiny of the unevangelized, by which persons who have never even heard of a particular revelation might be harshly punished for not following its dictates.

4. The analogy of Russell's teapot argues that the burden of proof for the existence of God lies with the theist rather than the atheist.

5. The argument from poor design contests the idea that God created life on the basis that lifeforms, including humans, seem to exhibit poor design.

The argument from design claims that a complex or ordered structure must be designed. A god that is responsible for the creation of a universe would be at least as complicated as the universe that it creates. Therefore, it too must require a designer. And its designer would require a designer also, ad infinitum. The argument for the existence of god is then a logical fallacy with or without the use of special pleading. A theory that points out that God does not provide an origin of complexity is The Ultimate **Boeing 747** gambit.

FIFTH CHAPTER

It's already lunch. Link-Leaping delivered on the time-wasting promise in abundance; the hours of the day have disappeared like tears in rain (that's from *Bladerunner*). I am divided, however. On the one hand I feel greatly satisfied by my new discovery, a fresh new tool to quell the office boredom, but on the other, I notice it hasn't left me unaffected. As I sit on the stone ledge that marks off the square in front of the office building, I think about God. I eat my vending-machine sandwich, and I can't help but think about him. I watch people come and go: some sit and eat hurried little lunches, but mostly they come and go, and in the midst of them all, like a single small, confused sperm in a wallop of an orgasm, I can't stop my thoughts. It's like having to go to the bathroom really bad. I clinch and squeeze, but in the end my mind prevails. Is God just another name for inner peace? Is God looking down at us right now, laughing? Those questions lead me into religion, and it's not long before I'm caught in a diarrhea of ponderations. God, religion, belief. I don't do it, honestly, I don't. It's my mind. By the time my vending-machine sandwich is down to the last bite I have reached a conclusion. It's utterly clear and vivid, the way I'd expect an alcoholic would see the truth as he sobers up for a second and realizes he's fucked up his whole life. Riddle me this, riddle me that, God is …

I'm the salsa in the sauce. I'm the whupass in the can. I'm the spinning motion of the world. I'm the little parts on an airplane, the ones you don't see but that are there, underneath the paint and the smooth steel, holding it all together.

....

I'm the ribbon in a girl's hair, flapping in the wind as she dances on the piazza with the other children. Their black shoes go clippety-clapp on the stones, the same stones horses trampled with their hooves a hundred years ago.

....

I'm the mothball hanging amongst centuries of clothes in the attic of Raffles Hotel in Singapore. I am the closet, too.

....

I'm the hook caught in the fleshy kiss-shaped mouth of a sea bass. I'm the empty beer cans on the bottom of the boat.

....

I'm the rusty ladder climbing up a brick-walled house, reaching, stretching for the clean blue sky above.

....

I'm not the cotton-clustered clouds with flat bottoms and curly tops roaming the skies. I'm not the pigeon cooing in a nest atop the city, but I am the wood, the net, and the nails keeping it captive and safe from the hawk – who, by the way, I'm not.

....

I'm the pearl inside an oyster, only after, when it lies curled up like a poisonous snake ready to strike, in a shop window in Hong Kong.

I'm the mechanical heart that beats inside Grandpa. I'm also the remote control and the security gate in the airport that can kill him.

....

I'm the shiny, colorful wrapping, silvery on the inside, that lines miles and miles of shelf space throughout stores all over the world, also found floating in the shallow and dirty waters on the coast outside a city.

....

I'm the trees, and I am the paper neatly stacked and bundled into books.

....

I am a needle pushing through frail yellow membrane, looking for a vein in an arm full of empty holes. I'm not the heart that almost stops when it hits. I'm not. But I am the dope running a short crazy sprint through the inflamed red arteries.

....

I'm the leather sandal lifting and falling from a girl's heel as she crosses the boardwalk.

....

I'm the knife that cuts open the breast and spills its blood like nectar from a ripe peach. I'm the small wad of silicone stuffed inside. Stuffed inside the gape to satisfy the hungry beast.

....

I'm the quartz-crystal image of the numbers 12:58 floating in the grey pool of a wristwatch on a Thursday in Taiwan.

....

I'm the glass window through which you see a woman and two men on a bed. I'm the bed and also the shining polka-dot vibrator.

....

I'm not love, that which bubbles in a pot on a fire inside the heart. I'm not that.

I'm the bullet passing through soft skin, leaving a gaping hole of fire on the other side.

I'm the umbrella stuck at an angle in the white sand on Stromboli. I'm not the shade, and I'm not the volcano juggling red fireball oranges in the night.

I'm the anchor breaking the surface and crashing into the sea, sinking through emerald blue spectra, but the millions of tiny white bubbles racing towards the surface I am not.

I'm the paper dragon jostling about in the wind, spastic, connected to a thin string above Golden Gate Park.

I'm the white fluff inside Teddy Bear's ears.

I'm all the green garbage pails in the world. I'm all the rest, too.

I am the glue under a sticker of a smiling pirate smeared on the bumper of a hippie-painted Volkswagen bus speeding down Vine Street.

I am a cylindrical cork holding two worlds apart. One wet and hazy, the other cold and grey.

I am spokes on a wheel, but I'm not dust on a car.

I am a necklace carrying Jesus on the cross.

I am the pulp of an orange dripping down a paralyzed, stubbly cheek at the hospice.

I am a wicker basket filled with stones made smooth by the sea, standing on the counter of a women's restroom.

I am the piece of rope between a man with violently flailing legs and a wood beam over a century old.

I am all kinds of boxes and all kinds of bags.

I am vulcanized rubber, and I am lubricant with raspberry scent. But I am not an orgasm.

I am the holes in a spaghetti drainer, and I am the spaghetti.

I am the platinum-blonde bleach Marilyn applied that day in March, wearing plastic gloves.

I am this and I am that. No matter where you go or what you do, I'll be there. I have my hands in nearly everything, but I *am* not everything. I've been in safe-deposit boxes and shoes, between boobs, under stacks of books, in noses, under armpits, even in assholes. I go by many names: some call me Buck, some call me Bill, but who am I really other than a figment of your imagination? I only exist because you believe in me. All right, you got me. I am money.

That's right. My little lunchtime revelation tells me that God is money, money is God. It's the only thing that makes sense. In fact, it makes perfect bloody sense. If God is money, we obey and worship Him, and whoever says enough prayers and is willing to do anything to be in His presence will bathe in riches. If God is money, God is everywhere. He is in each taxicab, in each pants pocket, in the outstretched hands of beggars, under buns on the hot-dog vendor's cart. If it's not yet completely so, then let's make it so. Right now. If we all just agree, then we'd have a set of rules everyone can live by. Dollars and cents, they will be our scriptures. Yen and rubles, praise the Lord. Euros and pesos from here on into eternity.

In a couple of minutes my lunch break will be over, and the fact that there's not already a world religion called Money baffles me. Why hasn't anyone with a longer lunch break written down the prophecy of Money? It would be a religion with guidelines anyone could follow. No difficult ten commandments to obey, only the one: the more you own, the closer you are to God. The less you have, the less you are. We'd make department stores into our churches, banks into our temples. We'd bury our dead in British sports cars. Children would learn from an early age what was expected of them, and each individual walking the surface of the earth would know clearly what the point of it all was. No more disillusion, searching for the true meaning. It would be right there, printed on cotton-fiber paper. A chasing-the-buck religion. And best of all, anyone can join. It would be free.

I pull out a quarter from my pocket and look at it. "If only you could speak, my friend," I whisper to it, "you'd be king." I flip the quarter upwards as hard as I can and watch it soar into the sky. After what seems to be half of a forever it lands with a soft jingle in the middle of the square. Not even twenty seconds later a prosperous-looking man in a suit bends down quickly and snatches it up. "Hallelujah, brother," I whisper his way and hurry back to my desk.

Perhaps it's God, perhaps it's the sandwich, but when I'm back in my rectangular prism I don't feel in tip-top shape. I'm leaning towards the sandwich. Vending-machine food comes with a predicament: stuff that isn't circulated often runs the risk of being really old, and stuff that is circulated sells out. I manage to chug through a couple of ads before I have to rush-walk to the bathroom, prepared to be sick. There in the darkness I grasp for a straw and come up with the only working form of new-aginess I can think of. It's another thing left behind by my ex, and I make a mental note to reflect about all the ways she is still in my life – as soon as I feel better.

Forget for a moment what you know. Forget everything. Think only of a black dot. Close your eyes and see it from within, the same way you see when you dream. See the black dot, solid and large, just sitting there. This is all you know. You know about nothing else but the black dot. Now, see it move out, away from you. First it moves slowly, then faster and faster, until it's so far away, so little, you can't see it anymore. Now open your eyes and feel the emptiness.

It works. Whatever spiritual deity has come to my rescue, the writing is on the wall. And through the darkness it reads: the ads. Of course. I am sickened by the sludge I have to crawl through. I can't recall the specifics of the culprits right now, and I don't want to. I just want the black dot to keep the evil forces at bay for a little while longer.

There are just so many of them. I'll simply pick two off the Brobdingnagian pile at the top of my mind. And they couldn't be better suited, for if there are two expressions I really hate, they are *Living life to the fullest* and *Life is what you make of it*. Let's break them down.

Living life to the fullest

To understand this I must try to understand its opposite. Is it possible to live your life only half-full? Days are six hours long; taxes are cut 50 percent, the flight to L.A. is only three hours? Maybe I'm missing the point, but that doesn't sound all that bad, if you ask me.

The fault lies mainly with that tear-jerking 1990s Abercrombie-and-Fitch-sponsored *Dead Poets Society*. Although what jerked those tears wasn't the main message of the movie, which was that theater and nineteenth-century literature can be, gosh, really great. Rather, it was that this was Robin Williams's last good performance in a movie. What's worse, however, is the wreckage it brought on. Suddenly every kid between fifteen and twenty-five learned that the thing of utmost importance, besides having a really nice scarf and duffle coat, was sucking the marrow from life. Without constraint everybody started using it, seize the day, like some bad schoolyard rhyme. Living life to the fullest. And although we may think we know what it means (boredom), and we shun it like European peasants used to shun the plague, the phrase has simply become a logo, fit only for declaring your fast-food spirituality to the world.

Life is what you make of it

If there's one thing life has shown us it's that it doesn't care one iota what we think. We try to put a leash on it: we plan, we study, we set goals and nurture dreams into obsessions. But life will either chomp through that leash with one swift bite and leave you there, all alone and frightened, or it will tear through the park with the force of a hundred elephants, and all you can do is hang on for dear life.

Life, despite your best intentions, puts you where it will. Like a bully at school, it sizes you up the moment you arrive, and from then on it has its way with you. You are in the grips of life every waking hour and every unconscious hour. You are life's bitch. Some of us are even life's bitch's bitch. Life is what you make of it? You are what life makes of you. You better believe it.

When I turn on the light the black dot is still there. I have concentrated so hard on it that I can still trace the outline hovering in front of my eyes. But it worked, or perhaps it was my mind's ranting. It doesn't matter. What matters is that I keep my stomach turned the right way and my gastric juices safe inside. When the black dot finally disappears I scuffle back to my desk, moving in the manner of one who has just taken a massive dump.

On my way home from work I end up stalking another girl. I'm not sure why I do these things – it's not like I plan them, but when opportunity knocks I feel I have to let who-the-fuck in. This time, who-the-fuck is a squirrel-faced girl with Uggs. On my way to the subway I walk right into her subtle cloud of perfume; it encapsulates me in the scent of something summer, and right away I am hooked. She is shorter than me, chest-high, and the way she walks, careful and carefree, treading across the asphalt in her soft boots, impresses and entices me to no end. In a different place, a wholly different life, I'd be a lion, mouth watering, stalking a grazing herbivore.

I keep within the cloud of scent – that means five steps behind, for anyone without stalking experience. It's odd: I don't feel like a creep because I know my intentions are pure. Yet at the same time I'm disappointed in myself. It's a foregone conclusion that this will lead nowhere, following a strange girl on the streets of New York. In the hopes of what? That suddenly a meteorite will crush the intersection before us, leaving her hanging from the edge of the gaping hole so I can come to her rescue? All the naysayers tell me that, theoretically, it *could* happen. All the yea-sayers say that, theoretically, *anything* can happen. On the spur of the moment

I decide to ignore the yea-sayers and push myself outside my comfort zone. I will approach her.

On the corner of 47th and the Avenue of the Americas she turns left, and for a second she disappears around the corner wall. I jump-skip forward, ready to put my finger on her shoulder, and suddenly stumble right into her. "Hey, buddy, watch it, buddy." The collision tumbles her even further into his embrace. The boyfriend. What a creep, waiting like that around a corner. I hum and I shrug, I may even hawk, and I keep walking east although I really should be heading west to get to my subway station. All the way home I feel pretty dumb. Like the universe has singled me out to star in one of its jokes. I think that's the main reason I decide to do it, what I've never done before. That, and because I feel it's time I put an end to the stalking. I log into the dating site.

Everybody else does it, why can't I? "I took the stairs instead of the elevator today, so I'll take two of the small cakes," the fat lady pants. It's really too easy to justify your actions.

I sit at my kitchen table and for the first time in my life I write a profile for myself, as myself (sort of). Funny thing is, as I write it I realize just how easy it is. I don't have to think about what I'm doing and what comes out is one very smart – enticing, even – description of quite the interesting young man, with just enough edge, but not so over-the-top I become a clown. After I've put up a few unidentifiable pictures and reread the whole thing, I don't recognize myself. Because I'm no longer myself. I've gone from being a stalker to becoming a polished version of the single woman's dream partner. Tender, yet with firm opinions, smart but compassionate, striving but relaxed, fit but fun-loving, funny and serious. Short and sweet, it's the Botoxed version of a Belgian Blue enhanced dating profile. *I've created a dating monster,* I think as I post myself and then spend the rest of the evening trying to forget what I've just done.

What's your story, morning glory?

Diane, my rectangular friend, is waiting when I get to work today. She tells me all about her leaping, how she started on Michael J. Fox and ended on the Isthmus of Panama. It's quite the leap, whatever the hell an isthmus is. I tell her about Coney Island, the rabbits, the dwarfs, giants, pretzels, and whatnot, and let her know I'm off with a boom today: Boeing 747. Can't help but feel we are two explorers set for the unknown. We have entered the jungle, and now we are forced to cut our way out while harvesting oh so much of the sweet spice of modern life that we call irreverence. I fasten the straps of my pith helmet and bid her farewell.

BOEING 747

The Boeing 747 is a widebody commercial airliner and cargo transport, often referred to by the nickname *Jumbo Jet* or *Queen of the Skies.*

Boeing agreed to deliver the first 747 to Pan Am by the end of 1969. The delivery date left 28 months to design the aircraft, which was two-thirds the normal time. The schedule was so fast paced that the people who worked on it were given the nickname "The Incredibles"

As of September 2010, the 747 has been involved in 124 accidents or incidents, including 49 hull-loss accidents, resulting in 2,852 fatalities. The 747 has been in 31 hijackings, which caused 25 fatalities.

VC-25 – This aircraft is the U.S. Air Force Very Important Person (VIP) version of the 747-200B. The U.S. Air Force operates two of them in VIP configuration as the VC-25A. Tail numbers 28000 and 29000 are popularly known as **Air Force One**.

AIR FORCE ONE

The "Air Force One" call sign was created after a 1953 incident involving a flight carrying President Dwight D. Eisenhower entering the same airspace as a commercial airline flight using the same call sign.

Air Force One is the official air traffic control call sign of any United States Air Force aircraft carrying the **President of the United States**.

PRESIDENT OF THE UNITED STATES

The President of the United States is the head of state and head of government of the United States.

Article II, Section 1, Clause 5 of the Constitution sets the principal qualifications one must meet to be eligible to the office of president. A president must:

-be a natural born citizen of the United States;

-be at least thirty-five years old;

-have been a permanent resident in the United States for at least fourteen years.

The president earns a $400,000 annual salary, along with a $50,000 annual expense account, a $100,000 non-taxable travel account and $19,000 for entertainment.

The White House in Washington, D.C. serves as the official place of residence for the president; he is entitled to use its staff and facilities, including medical care, recreation, housekeeping, and security services. Naval Support Facility Thurmont, popularly known as Camp David, is a mountain-based military camp in Frederick County, Maryland used as a country retreat and for high alert protection of the president and his guests. Blair House, located adjacent to the Old Executive Office Building at the White House Complex and Lafayette Park, is a complex of four connected townhouses exceeding 70,000 square feet (6,500 m2) of floor space which serves as the president's official guest house and as a secondary residence for the president if needed.

For ground travel, the president uses the presidential state car, which is an armored limousine built on a heavily modified Cadillac-based chassis. The president also uses a United States Marine Corps helicopter, designated Marine One when the president is aboard.

The United States Secret Service is charged with protecting the sitting president and his family. As part of their protection, presidents, first ladies, their children and other immediate family members, and other prominent persons and locations are assigned **Secret Service codenames**.

SECRET SERVICE CODENAMES

The United States Secret Service uses code names for U.S. presidents, first ladies, and other prominent persons and locations.

The use of such names was originally for security purposes and dates to a time when sensitive electronic communications were not routinely encrypted; today, the names simply serve for purposes of brevity, clarity, and tradition. The Secret Service does not choose these names, however. The White House Communications Agency assigns these names.

The WHCA is headquartered at Anacostia Navy Yard and consists of six staff elements and seven organizational units. WHCA also has supporting detachments in Washington, D.C. and various locations throughout the United States of America.

According to established protocol, 'good' codewords are unambiguous words that can be easily pronounced and readily understood by those who transmit and receive voice messages by radio or telephone regardless of their native language. Traditionally, all family members' code names start with the same letter.

Richard Nixon - Searchlight
Pat Nixon – Starlight

Jimmy Carter - Deacon
Rosalynn Carter – Dancer

Ronald Reagan - Rawhide
Nancy Reagan – Rainbow

George W. Bush - Tumbler or Trailblazer
Laura Bush – Tempo

Barack Obama - Renegade
Michelle Obama - Renaissance

John F. Kennedy - Lancer
Jacqueline Kennedy – Lace

JACQUELINE KENNEDY

Jacqueline Lee Bouvier Kennedy Onassis (July 28, 1929 – May 19, 1994 was the wife of the 35th President of the United States, John F. Kennedy, and served as First Lady during his presidency from 1961 until his assassination in 1963. She is remembered for her contributions to the arts and historic preservation, her style and elegance.

Bouvier married Kennedy on September 12, 1953, at St. Mary's Church in Newport, Rhode Island. The wedding cake was created by Plourde's Bakery in Fall River, Massachusetts. The wedding dress, now housed in the Kennedy Library in Boston, Massachusetts, were created by designer Ann Lowe of New York City.

A week after the assassination, Jacqueline was interviewed in Hyannisport on November 29 by Theodore H. White of Life magazine. In that session, she compared the Kennedy years in the White House to King Arthur's mythical Camelot, commenting that the President often played the title song of Lerner and Loewe's musical recording before retiring to bed.

In June 1968 when her brother-in-law Robert F. Kennedy was assassinated, she came to fear for her life and that of her children, saying "If they're killing Kennedys, then my children are targets...I want to get out of this country." On October 20, 1968 she married Aristotle Onassis, a wealthy, Greek shipping magnate, who was able to provide the privacy and security she needed for herself and her children.

The wedding took place on Skorpios, Onassis's private island in the Ionian Sea, Greece. After her marriage to Onassis, Jacqueline lost her Secret Service protection and her **Franking Privilege**, both of which are entitlements to a widow of the President of the United States.

FRANKING PRIVILEGE

"Privilege" franking is a personally pen-signed or printed facsimile signature of a person with a "franking privilege" such as certain government officials (especially legislators) and others designated by law or Postal Regulations. This allows the letter or other parcel to be sent without the application of an actual postage stamp.

In Italy, mail sent to the President used to be free of charge, but this franking privilege was abolished in 1999.

In **New Zealand**, individuals writing to a Member of Parliament can do so without paying for postage.

NEW ZEALAND

The indigenous Māori language name for New Zealand is Aotearoa, commonly translated as *land of the long white cloud*.

During its long isolation New Zealand developed a distinctive fauna dominated by birds, a number of which became extinct after the arrival of humans and the mammals they introduced.

Until the arrival of humans, 80% of the land was forested. A diverse range of megafauna inhabited the forests, including the flightless moas (now extinct), four species of kiwi, the kakapo and the takahē, all endangered by human actions. Unique birds capable of flight included the **Haast's eagle**, which was the world's largest bird of prey.

HAAST'S EAGLE

Haast's Eagle (*Harpagornis moorei*) was a species of massive eagles that once lived on the South Island of New Zealand. The species was the largest eagle known to have existed.

Haast's Eagles preyed on large, flightless bird species, including the moa, which was up to fifteen times the weight of the eagle. It is estimated to have attacked at speeds up to 80 km/h (50 mph), often seizing its prey's pelvis with the talons of one foot and killing with a blow to the head or neck with the other. Its size and weight indicate a bodily striking force equivalent to a cinder block falling from the top of an eight-storey building. Its large beak also could be used to rip into the internal organs of its prey and death then would have been caused by blood loss.

The Haast's Eagle became extinct about 1400 CE, when its major food sources, the moa, were hunted to extinction by humans living on the island.

Haast's Eagle was first classified by **Julius von Haast** in the 1870s.

JULIUS VON HAAST

Sir Johann Franz "Julius" von Haast (May 1, 1824 – August 16, 1887) was a German geologist. In 1858 he traveled to New Zealand to report on the suitability of the colony for German emigrants. He carried on important researches with reference to the occurrence of Moa and other extinct flightless birds, and he discovered **gold** and coal in Nelson.

GOLD

Gold is a chemical element with the symbol Au (from Latin: aurum "gold", originally "shining dawn") and an atomic number of 79. Gold metal is dense, soft, shiny and the most malleable and ductile pure metal known.

A total of 165,000 tonnes of gold have been mined in human history, as of 2009. This is roughly equivalent to about 8,500 m³, or a cube 20.4 m on each side.

The largest gold depository in the world is that of the U.S. Federal Reserve Bank in New York, which holds about 3% of all the gold ever mined, as does the similarly laden **U.S. Bullion Depository** at Fort Knox.

SIXTH CHAPTER

Her name is Cat, with a *C*. Her three profile pictures include a total of two of her dog, Thirty, but by the time I have based my decision to meet her on the remaining picture – not that her profile text is unimportant, but as they say, brains only get you so far – I still don't know about any dog named Thirty. We are meant to have dumplings somewhere on the east side of Chinatown, but the streets are displaced and our minds seem to be also, so after soliciting the unrewarding blocks for a while we decide to ditch the dumplings and head for a friend of Cat's. We literally have only to cross the street, enter a dingy once-upon-a-time green-painted door, climb up two flights of stairs that lean heavily to one side, and we are at the party. Cat is an actress, a student, a painter, like any young gal in New York aspiring to be everything, but statistically more likely to get pregnant or to die at a crosswalk. First she tells me she works as a stripper and waits for shock to ripple across my face, but she is such a terrible liar that a ripple runs across my face only when she tells me about her acting.

She is a transplant from Pennsylvania, the state that (for anyone not from the U.S.) is about as useless and anonymous as Slovakia is in Europe. Her features are frail and nymphlike, boasting not much color and few distinct features, but with an air of royalty and some hidden knowledge of times past. She is wearing jeans tucked into worn cowboy boots, a T-shirt that looks tailor-made, and a scarf hanging open around her neck. While looking for the dumpling place we spoke only about matters regarding the dumpling place, but at the party we finally stop moving around, and by a window at the end of a long room we sit on a ledge with our plastic cups and she tells me all about Thirty. He is a mutt. A picture is produced, and I wonder whether Apple would have ever built the iPhone had they known how many pets and babies were to be shoved in people's faces thereafter. But I have to say, I've seen much uglier dogs. He really does look like a mutt, though, an imperfect match of breeds, as if someone had taken two dogs, chopped them in half, and stuck the different parts together. His front part is bulldoggish and heavyset, featuring a round face with pudgy cheeks, but his back part is slim and long-haired, a wiener-dog body, and the whole creation is so remarkable that I for the moment can't loathe her for showing it to me.

She says we can see her apartment from where we sit, and I lean out as she points up and over to a window in the building across the street. I'm not sure if I should take this as an invite, but the subject drifts beyond my control, and I can't get it back to her apartment, no matter how I try. We broach the subject of online dating. I say it's a totally new thing for me, and from my perspective it's a fact, not a lie. She asks me what it was about her profile that caught my interest, and I answer that it was Thirty. "Anyone with a dog, in fact," I continue, and I feel the devil's laughter tickle the bottom of my feet, "all pet-owners are more in touch with their feelings. They are proven to be more compassionate people. That, and I really liked your smile," I say.

The party happens all around us, music playing, feet shuffling, laughter cascading through the beats, and right then and there I sense that feeling. We are inside a bubble in all the surrounding commotion, and nothing can penetrate it. I've felt it before, but like the subject of her apartment, it drifts away from me before I can pin it down. Without the bubble it's back to being just a party with a stranger showing me pictures of her dog, and I fail to suppress a yawn and say *it's been a long day, I had a good time,* and we leave the party together. I walk her around the block, across the street to her house and leave her with a hug and, as it happens, a swift lip-buff on the cheek that I, on the train ride home, have a hard time classifying into any of the dating endings so far known to me. And that's what really bugs me the most about the date: the unclassifiable termination of it. It bugs the hell out of me.

I talked to Cat about myself as a writer. It's a delusion under which we all suffer, this creating what we want by saying it. It crosses boundaries and spans gorges in perfect harmony and connects all us lowly humans. It works in online dating: in order to get your order exactly as you wish it to be you have to write in detail what it is you are looking for. "A tall, dark, expert macchiato-making, lavender softener–user, chest hair groomed, from out of state, in the legal profession, piercings ok but no tattoos, love kids but must not have them, beer-battered, wafer-crusted, nudist-loving 40-ish something. If you are out there, reply by neon sign." As long as you say it, as long as you are precise and detailed enough in your wishes, they may just become true. I tell her I'm a writer because when someone asks you what you do you need something heavy and impressive to sock them with. Something that takes their breath away, or at least leaves an indentation of sorts.

And I did write a book, but truth be told, the only time I actually felt like a writer wasn't when I finished it, or when it came from the printer, or even when it was plastered in every literary blog and magazine around the world. It was for but a brief period on that day when I met J. D. Salinger's son. We were in a conference room above many other rooms, high above the once-upon-a-time grit and dirt on the street below. New York, the polished apple. She always reminds me of that fairy tale by Hans Christian Andersen, the one about the ugly duckling that thought he was a swan. New York was once a duck, long before my time, even up until and briefly into my time, and she quacked and shat all over the floor. She was constantly knocking things over, flapping those wings carelessly, as if the whole world was on its toes for her, knowing when to, well, duck. She was brutal and daring, even feculantly revolting at times, but she was charming. She was a duck that would charm your pants off, then shit on them and buffet your face with her wings, but you'd take it all because of that charm.

Now she's become a prima donna, snotty and stuck-up, with a constant snarl about her mouth. Now she pirouettes between the kitchen and the living room, wings tucked in tightly, hardly moving a feather. Nothing's knocked over, she shits in a golden box by the window that is cleaned once a day, and the gleam that was once in her eyes is gone. She knows it, too, but she can do nothing but continue on, pretending the past will catch up, hoping the future will bring gifts of change.

And so there I was, in the fancy conference room high above the once-upon-a-time golden-smiled charmer. The son was already there, tall and grayish, with a very large head. In fact, his head was the first thing I noticed, and afterward it was the one thing that lived liveliest in my memory. One lawyer, two lawyers, three lawyers, the son's giant head, me and the book, all crammed into that conference room. Terms were flung, eyebrows first raised and then furrowed and bent. It was the waltz of the eyebrows, and I accepted the invitation and joined the peculiar dance of facial hair without thinking twice. And there, at the end of our sitting down together as adults, discussing the being and possible unbeing of my book, a question is raised that stops all the eyebrows in a stroke. They hang there from faces, from the son's large, fleshy face, like quivering squirrels waiting for a bear to pass underneath. "You are a writer. You have written it, and you are a writer. What else do you want?"

I could say nothing. That's all I want, and that's what I felt right there in that conference room. I didn't even care that the once so ugly but charming duck had become a boring, unflattering swan. I didn't care that eyebrows bounced and slithered across their mugs. All I cared about was that feeling, the one I had been chasing. I was finally a writer, for someone other than myself had claimed it, and that was all that mattered. I said not another word and only sat there with that feeling, nurturing it, observing it, and finally embracing it. I nodded, and we parted ways, nothing resolved, nothing decided, but everything changed. It's a blessing when it happens, and it happens to most of us, the christening; we exit through the mouth of a machine that slaps us, wet and with a thud, with a label. I am a police officer. I am a technophile and a freedom fighter. I am a muffin-lover. I am a writer. Everywhere are labels, a multifarious horde on each of us, one for each attribute, feeling, and desire. I wish we could see them in plain view. Some are more visible than others, but what a world it would be if all labels were Post-it notes stuck to our foreheads. It would be a librarian's dream. And that, this all, is why I told her I am a writer. Because I intended to indent her wildly, and because I wear my labels proudly.

All I write these days are the profiles at work and the messages to Diane. For a while I entertained thoughts of starting a blog, if only to divert the stream of words welling inside. But I keep the dams shut. I know I would only loathe myself if I succumbed to the tribe of blog-vampires. Surely I can't be the only one who think blogs are nothing but digital screams for help. They are the most readily available listen-to-me's of the twenty-first century, socially and economically leveled suicide notes. A desperate attempt to cage in a bit of the ever-collapsing universe. When immigrants came to America in the 1900s the brave ones staked their claims out west, in a barren land filled with Indians and rattlesnakes. It was a way of survival, and although it is a far cry from our modern society, if you fail to see the similarities in the workings of the human mind you are blind. Bloggers too wish to stake out their ground. They say: this is my land and on it I shall grow whatever I fancy and I will build myself a house to protect my family and I will dance around naked in it if I so choose. And on my land and in my house my rules apply, and I will declare what is just and what is wrong, and if you don't like it you can get the hell out. I have opinions and I will grow them like onions all over the soddy patch in the back, and perhaps in the front too. This is my voice and if I scream loud enough maybe you can hear me. This is me carving a sliver from the tree of life, if only for purpose of showing you, when I'm gone, that I was once here.

I just couldn't live with the burden of a blog. To know it was out there, floating around like a strayed child without any parental reins, my own flesh and blood waiting to be picked up by the first pederast with a soul tormented enough to read my thoughts. A blog is an autopsy of cognitive content, and although some carry it out with utter honesty, it is still a slaughter best kept private.

There, there, I know you have them. The kicker is, we all do. Thoughts and opinions are not worth a piss because so few are original, and what good is sharing with the masses that which once came from that very flock of sheep?

On top of it all, my ex has joined the forces of the digital cockroaches, but I don't feel like talking about it right now.

Bri stops by my rectangular prism today. After what can only have been hours of messaging Diane about my recent link-leaping adventures, I hear the tap of fingernails on the painted plywood wall, a sound I henceforth shall connect only with Bri and with a cat ripping the wallpaper from an unsuspecting owner's living room corner. To my good fortune I have just started on a string of new profiles, and I turn with the faked annoyance of a busy worker who can think of nothing more repulsive than being disturbed while busily pouring his blood into the Corporation. I must have made a good impression for Bri hesitates, scrunches her eyebrows, and asks if she is disturbing me. I take on the understanding, helpful role, shrug my shoulders and let out a sigh that says more than any words about the pressures of my workload. I assure her she isn't imposing. Right away I sense that something is different. Although I've seen her up close many times before, this is the first time I see weakness shining through. She acts as though she is, if not nervous, then at least anxious about something. Just before she finally decides my prism isn't the place for it and, with one crook of her finger and about thirty feet of carpeted industrial floor, I find myself inside Bri's office, I realize what it is. The thundercloud is gone.

I have no idea why I'm here. The possibility that I am about to get fired both tickles me with anticipation and sends shivers of anxiety down my cowardly spine. I begin running through excuses in my head. I sift through a Rolodex filled with self-justifications, alibis and possible scapegoats. Finally, when she speaks, I can't believe my ears. I hesitate, and she notices. Sweet talk commences, and it's not just the words "as a friend" that finally push me over the edge. It makes perfect sense, putting up a profile for Bri.

Not only will the entire company benefit from the success of Bri finding a partner through her own service, which she claims is the whole reason for the project (even though I sense there is more behind it), it will give me something weighty to do – more weighty than weightless, anyway. But what really surprised me was the way she looked at me; it wasn't just the eyes of a boss asking her employee to carry out an order. Through her eyes I got a glimpse of her inner sanctuary, and what I saw there, what she wasn't fast enough to hide, was the snoot of a lonely little creature. It was only very brief – then the shutters to her soul came down with a kablamm! and the whites of her eyes were once again impenetrable and her expression professionally focused. Anyway, we are having lunch tomorrow so I can gather what little information she is prepared to give me as fodder for creating her profile, and although I bet anybody else on the floor would have been thrilled and proud and whatnot of all those yummy feelings that describe the general excitement of life, I can't help but feel like a traitor. I decide not to tell Diane, and I definitely won't talk about it with tonight's date, the fact that I'm about to sleep with the enemy.

We meet outside an oyster place on MacDougal Street. Her name is Kate Susan, she is from Australia and she likes oysters, books, and laughing, and I thought that was as good match as any. She also has perky breasts with nipples that try to burrow through her shirt. However, we have to make do with laughter, at least for the time being, because as it turns out the oyster shack is closed due to an unconfirmed tide-related problem, and she is not yet drunk enough to show me her nipples. Instead we head into the West Village to look for another oyster joint. We find one on Cornelia Street and by the time we sit down I already think of her as my sister. Not as a relative per se, but our words flow with such ease; we are talking about people like we've both known them for years and about places like we've both spent our childhood summers there. Like the middle period between childhood and adulthood has made us grow tired of them, but we have now discovered that they glow with nostalgia. Of course, thirty minutes ago I had never met her, but it is one of those things that just happens, I suppose, when you run into a person who is attached to the same strings of life as you.

She drinks champagne and gets bubbly, and I tell the waitress she is pregnant and that's why she is slouching. The waitress, either a baby-killer or not a fan of biology, brings us more champagne, and now we tell anyone who wants to listen that Kate is pregnant and that's why she is lying down across two chairs. I lay down on my side, too, and we see each other's faces under the table. We are two kids left home alone while our parents are away, and we explore the underworld with jovial excitement, not bothering to sit up straight even when the waitress brings in the dessert. Afterward we walk it off by moving eastward, and Kate pulls a camera out of her purse and begins taking pictures of seemingly random things. This way it takes us ten minutes to cross over to each new avenue, and when we reach Second Avenue we are both tired and Kate's camera is filled with senseless depictions of flowers, bricks, pigeons, hats, and dogs. From Second we turn south, and that's when I realize, although I had already suspected it, under the excess of joviality, that we will never be intimate.

I walk in silence next to her, and I think that I can never lay my hand on her that way or push her hair to one side and lean in to kiss those lips. We enter McNally's bookstore, an oasis of groove in a sea of crap. A café crams into one corner and the rest is books. We order a chai from the lady behind the counter, a bookstore café countess, proud and statuesque, ruling firmly over her fifty-square-foot kingdom from behind a desk lined with jars of cookies. Over chai I sense that Kate is expecting a move. She locks her eyes to mine, then clips them away, almost violently, as if they otherwise risked sticking to me permanently. I get fidgety and keep spinning my cup slowly around. A dark, wet circle forms under it, but I keep it spinning. The fidgetiness is contagious, and soon Kate begins as well. She twirls her keychain, putting it on the table and snaking it in symmetrical shapes. I hold my ground and lead the talk into the area of books, of anything I can think of but kissing my own sister, but soon enough the fidgeting catches up with us and we both understand the line has been crossed. Our smiles become harder, cast in porcelain, faced with the fact that this isn't the one. Without words we both get up at the same time; outside McNally's we part with a hug, and I think it's only appropriate that I walk in the opposite direction – this is, after all, how a parting is done – and I ambulate for a little while until the gloom is almost shaken off and I get on the train home.

It's a new day – new possibilities. Bri saw Björk eat here the other day, but I can't imagine why. It would have been perfect British Colonial – frail teacups, flowers in vases, white linen cloths – if it hadn't been for the guests. None wear ascot hats and monocles; they are just the same bunch of drab-looking American businesspeople in appropriately drab-looking suits. Bri is tapping her iPhone wildly, and as I look through the menu my contemplations on the nonexistence of American style make for a more interesting topic than any of the Asian-British fusion items printed before me. Finally Bri puts her phone down, and while we wait for our orders to arrive we practice what is commonly known as *small talk*. Bri has relapsed into the rarely seen, nervous version of her weaker self, and when the waiter brings in the pickled herring on rye bread it hits me. Could it be that Bri is interested in me, and this is why she made the lame excuse of asking me to write up her profile – to take me out to lunch? It's a shocking revelation created by my own mind, and I allow it to live only for a few moments, because nothing that happens during lunch supports my ludicrous thought. So little, in fact, that by the time we are done and on our way back to the office I have completely abandoned my wild theory. We make the last personal connection in the elevator, before the doors open, and afterward it is as if it never happened. She walks by my prism with hasty steps, without a word, and I saunter in, looking at no one, and sit right down in front of my computer.

I dabble with Bri's profile all afternoon. This responsibility grants me an even greater opportunity to slack off. All I have to do for some time to come is to manage my boss's profile, and that means I am temporarily excommunicated from the new-member decreet.

On my way home, at the edge of the street leading up to my apartment building, I come upon a young girl standing next to a jump rope tossed to the side of a giant heart chalked on the sidewalk. She is standing with her back to me; I'm guessing she is around ten, and the way she is leaning over something, curving her back and neck around it, I momentarily think she's sucking on a crack pipe. But when I pass her I see that it is only a plastic jar and spoon for blowing bubbles. For once innocence has prevailed. The girl lifts her head as I pass and flutters a long stream of bubbles at an angle into the air. They remain connected for a moment, a translucent string of pearls, but soon release from one another and diverge in all different directions. Some rise up further into the air, some flee out into the street, and others are crushed without a sound against the black-painted steel fence. Is this how nature speaks to us? I wonder about it as I keep one bubble with me the rest of the way home, not a real one but a purely metaphorical bubble. I am reminded of the date with Cat and of the fleeting feeling of being encapsulated. I remember it as something uniform for all my loves, enchantments, and even the briefest adornment of a stranger in a coffee shop. The bubble of love.

Once caught inside its rosy, shimmering walls, nothing else exists. But like all bubbles, the bubble of love is delicate and fleeting. It takes only the one careless probe for it to pop. Sometimes it lasts only a couple of minutes, as with Cat the other day. Other times it lasts longer: days, even weeks. But the longest that it can last (scientifically unproven but existentially demonstrated by me) is one month. I once began a novel that was called *The One-Month Man*. It was about a guy who could never succeed in keeping the novelty and mystery of love flowing longer than one month. Sure, he had relationships that were longer, but after the one-month doubt was planted in his mind it rooted quickly and spread to all areas of his psyche. One month is the honeymoon, a period when you don't let your guard down, you don't show your flaws, and you close the door the bathroom. But outside the bubble ordinary life waits patiently; it knows that no matter how uplifting or fancy, bubbles are bound to break.

The bubble reminds me, and I have no choice but to remember. I take a pen and paper and start making a list of all the ways she is still in my life. This is what I come up with:

The pirate skull bucket from IKEA
The potato-masher thingamabob
The affirmation magnets on the fridge
The black-dot mental exercise
An album of photographs from several small trips we made
A bunch of mental images that reappear at their own whim
Heartache
A few strands of hair
Dried flakes of dead skin

Somewhere out there, right now, she is sitting or walking or listening to music, not knowing that there are parts of her left here. I suppose that wherever we go we leave a tiny bit of ourselves behind. They say that 70 percent of the dust in our homes is really from our own dead skin, and perhaps that explains my lack of motivation for cleaning. Subconsciously I'm trying to hold on to her. But the thing that bothers me the most, what scares me more than a little, is that even with her – the one I'm missing so much that I'm counting crusts of her dead skin to ease my longing – even with her the bubble lasted only one month. I may be unsuitable for relationships, or worse, for love completely. I have felt it for a long time, but it's only now that I've come to realize that it might be permanent. After thirty-three years and one failed relationship after another.

I blame it on many things, but mostly I blame it on technology. We live in an age where technology has finally caught up to our imagination. Our fantasies are no longer animated, they are real. And this, this is the reason we are never truly satisfied.

But then, if I have the answer, why can't I stop looking? What use is there in meeting another and another and another to see if she fits into the mental cookie-cutter form life has shoved down my throat? I know what I want, and that very fact, that I know what I'm looking for, disturbs me to no end. I want a girl who makes me want to give up porn and the possibilities of fantasy. I want a girl who is attractive but not too attractive, but then again, not unattractive in any way, but still not overly attractive, at least not in the classical way, although it wouldn't hurt if her features can be clean and, well, classical. I want a pussy that squeaks like a rubber duck, but I don't want it to be made out of rubber. I want Christian values and a high moral code that can be tossed aside at will. I want that freakin´ cheese helmet Denis Leary ached for, the house, the kids, the car, the pool – the big kidney-shaped pool – the missile launcher, and I want to pop the cheese helmet on and just eat all day. Consumer love, this is what has happened to sonnets, chivalry, knights errant, Romeo and Juliet, oysters, and summer meadows. We scour the world for love like we scour the mall for the best price on sneakers. And just like with sneakers, the price we pay is exactly that what Mick and his senile rolling brothers sing about. I can't get no satisfaction.

SEVENTH CHAPTER

A new day has arrived, and with it a Santa's satchel of new possibilities. These aren't the exact words on my refrigerator door, but close to it. Yesterday is old news, yesterday never happened. There is only today, and today I shall try on a new pair of sneakers to see if they fit. But first, work.

Diane is already waiting when I get in.

Tell me about gold.

I tell her the basics of it, and as I do it strikes me how utterly insane the world we live in is. We are nothing but a species of giant ants that hurtle through space, astonishingly dumb, with only a flat perception of the universe. Once upon a time we decided that gold, perhaps because it glimmers, is the most desirable, and from that moment forth every waking hour has been spent in hunting it down and locking it in a vault.

U.S. BULLION DEPOSITORY

The United States Bullion Depository, commonly called Fort Knox, is a fortified vault building which is used to store a large portion of United States official gold reserves.

It holds about 4,603 tons (4,176 metric tonnes) of gold bullion. It is second in the United States only to the Federal Reserve Bank of New York's underground vault in Manhattan.

During World War II and on into the Cold War, until the invention of synthetic painkillers, a substantial supply of processed morphine and opium was kept in the Depository as a hedge against the United States being cut off from the sources of supply of raw opium.

Below the fortress-like structure lies the gold vault, which is lined with granite walls and which is protected by a blast-proof door that weighs 22 tons.

No single person is entrusted with the entire combination to the vault. Ten members of the Depository staff must dial separate combinations known only to them. Beyond the main vault door, smaller internal cells provide further protection. The small turret-like structures at the corners of the building are known to be firing positions for guards armed with **Thompson submachine guns.**

THOMPSON SUBMACHINE GUN

The Thompson is an American submachine gun, invented by John T. Thompson in 1919, that became infamous during the Prohibition era. It was a common sight in the media of the time, being used by both law enforcement officers and criminals.

The Thompson was also known informally as: the "TSMG", the "Tommy Gun", the "Trench Broom", the "Trench Sweeper", the "Chicago Piano", the "Chicago Typewriter", and the "Chopper".

It was often referred to as the "gun that made the twenties roar."

The Thompson achieved most of its early notoriety in the hands of Prohibition and Depression-era gangsters, motorized bandits and the lawmen who pursued them and in Hollywood films about their exploits, most notably in the **St Valentine's Day Massacre.**

ST VALENTINE'S DAY MASSACRE

The Saint Valentine's Day massacre is the name given to the murder of seven people as part of a prohibition era conflict between two powerful criminal gangs in Chicago, in 1929: the South Side Italian gang led by Al Capone and the North Side Irish gang led by Bugs Moran.

On the morning of Thursday, February 14, 1929, St. Valentine's Day, members of the North Side Gang were lined up against the rear inside wall of the (2122 North Clark Street) in the Lincoln Park neighborhood of Chicago's North Side, possibly by members of Al Capone's gang, possibly by gangsters hired from outside the city so they would not be recognized by their victims, or a combination of both.

Two of the shooters were dressed as Chicago police officers, and the others were dressed in long trenchcoats, according to witnesses who saw the "police" leading the other men at gunpoint out of the garage. When one of the dying men, Frank Gusenberg, was asked who shot him, he replied, "Nobody shot me" despite having 14 bullet wounds. Capone himself had arranged to be on vacation in Florida.

The only survivor in the warehouse was John May's **German Shepherd**, Highball.

GERMAN SHEPHERD

As part of the Herding group, the German Shepherd is a working dog developed originally for herding and guarding sheep.

In 1899 Max von Stephanitz, an ex-cavalry captain and former student of the Berlin Veterinary College, was attending a dog show when he was shown a dog named Hektor Linksrhein. Hektor was 1/4th wolf. Max was pleased with the strength of the dog and was so taken by the animal's intelligence and loyalty, that he purchased it immediately.

After he changed its name to Horand von Grafrath and founded the Verein für Deutsche Schäferhunde (Society for the German Shepherd Dog). Horand was declared to be the first German Shepherd Dog and was the first dog added to the society's breed register.

German Shepherds are considered to be the third most intelligent breed of dog, behind Border Collies and Poodles.

The bite of a German Shepherd Dog has a force of over 238 pounds (compared with that of a Rottweiler, 265-328 pounds of force, a Pitbull, 235 pounds of force, a Labrador Retriever, of approximately 125 pounds of force, or a human, of approximately 170 pounds of force)

Batman's dog **Ace the Bat-Hound** is a German Shepherd that appeared in the Batman comic books, initially in 1955, through 1964.

ACE THE BAT-HOUND

The comic book character Ace the Bat-Hound was the canine crime-fighting partner of Batman and Robin in DC Comics of the 1950s and 1960s.

Ace was a German Shepherd Dog originally owned by an engraver named John Wilker. He was found by Batman and Robin after his master was kidnapped by a gang of counterfeiters. Batman used Ace to try to locate Wilker. Because he had already placed a large number of "lost dog" announcements for Ace in his civilian identity of Bruce Wayne, he was concerned that anyone recognizing Ace (who had a prominent star-shaped marking on his forehead) might make the connection between Bruce Wayne and Batman. To forestall that problem, he hastily improvised a hood-like mask for the dog that incorporated the bat emblem as a **dog tag** dangling from Ace's collar.

DOG TAG

A dog tag is the informal name for the identification tags worn by military personnel.

Wearing of the tag is required at all times by soldiers in the field.

In the Vietnam War, American soldiers were allowed to place rubber silencers on their dog tags so the enemy would not hear the metallic clanking. Others chose to tape the two tags together with black tape. Still others chose to wear one tag around the neck and the other tag on the lace of one boot.

The tag is primarily used for the identification of dead and wounded along with providing religion (to provide for calling a

Catholic Priest or Jewish Rabbi for Last Rites) and essential basic medical information for the treatment of the latter, such as **blood type** and history of inoculations.

BLOOD TYPE

A total of 30 human blood group systems are now recognized by the International Society of Blood Transfusion (ISBT).

Almost always, an individual has the same blood group for life, but very rarely an individual's blood type changes through addition or suppression of an antigen in infection, malignancy, or autoimmune disease. An example of this rare phenomenon is the case of Demi-Lee Brennan, an Australian citizen, whose blood group changed after a liver transplant.

A popular belief in Japan is that a person's ABO blood type is predictive of their personality, character, and compatibility with others. Deriving from ideas of historical scientific racism, the theory reached Japan in a 1927 psychologist's report, and the militarist government of the time commissioned a study aimed at breeding better soldiers. The fad faded in the 1930s due to its unscientific basis. The theory has long since been rejected by scientists, but it was revived in the 1970s by **Masahiko Nomi**, a broadcaster who had no medical background.

MASAHIKO NOMI

Masahiko Nomi (July 18, 1925 - October 30, 1981) was a Japanese journalist who advocated Takeji Furukawa's idea of Japanese blood type theory of personality. He was also known as a **sumo** essayist.

Today I finish Bri's profile and present it to her for the first time. She approves of it and I have the thing online right after lunch. It contains just enough information to entice and seduce, but not so much as to reveal her real identity. I can tell she is pleased with my work, and oddly, I feel proud to have made her pleased. Again I get the notion that perhaps there's more behind her wish for a profile, and that, I conclude later that afternoon, is what spurs me to do something most unethical. Lately I have been seen wandering near the brink of things – it's an alarming development and surely a sign of despair – and what happens this afternoon only proves that. I send Bri's profile a message from my own steroid-pumped one.

On my way to yet another date (Ina, a Brazilian transplant working in the advertising industry and a bit of a ninnyhammer, residing in some small New Jersey commuter town), I have sort of an epiphany. Well, not really, it's smaller than an epiphany, it's the epiphany of an epiphany, or perhaps, the nail clippings from God that happen to land on my head. It happens in the elevator, where it is not unusual for similarly prophetic thoughts to reveal themselves. The elevator is a cocoon, a vertical portal to another dimension that takes us from one place and delivers us into another. Perhaps it's not so strange after all, to there harbour such thoughts. Maybe it's the silent whirring and the knowledge of soaring on a mere wire, or the lack of windows. Either way, the thought that comes to me as I descend to the ground in a controlled fall is about dreams and desire. The chasing we do in the game of life.

The
Game
of
Life

The game of life is played out on a big field. The purpose of the game is to chase a ball that appears in the distance. At sight of it we begin to run across the field, only there's something funny with the ball. It seems that even when you've caught it, you never really have it. The moment you lay your hands on it – *POOF!* – another, identical ball appears at the opposite end of the field. So you keep running towards the new ball, racing over the grassy mounds and muddy patches, so focused on the new ball that you have totally forgotten about the one you just caught, and when you have finally realized it, the new ball is gone too.

Billionaires, millionaires, businessmen, movie stars, oil-sheiks, supermodels, hip hoppers, investment bankers, bank robbers, politicians, taxi drivers, grocery-store workers, street peddlers, prostitutes, welfare-takers, factory assemblers, cleaners and bums, they are all on the field together, chasing the same ball. A field with unlimited acreage but a limited view. They chase for the same reasons, and if they would only stop for a moment and look around, take their eyes from the ball, they would see all these people running back and forth in every direction, their gazes locked on the distance, and they would realize how ridiculous it all was and how lonely they all really were. And then they would start running again.

This is the sickness of the world. The race you can't remember entering but, all of a sudden, you find yourself running anyway. Running for your life to get to the finish line, only to discover there never was one. Discovering you've been kept in the trick bag all along.

But what if life demands secrets and dreams that never come true? What if, in life, we need the illusion of the chase to motivate us to take another step, and another, and another? The greatest curse may very well be getting what you wish for. On the other hand, this is what people who have failed to reach their goals say.

At Penn Station the halls swarm with commuters of all human shapes and sizes. I join a line that wriggles slowly towards a section of ticketing machines. Somewhere there's a ballgame, a new restaurant, a stag night, an empty apartment, a wife and a set of twins, a pet iguana, a ward filled with patients, a ship without a captain. Everyone is going somewhere. The line snakes forward, and soon it's my turn. Every person around me carries a world inside their head. A complete set of longings and belongings perched on a moving sack of water and blood. Reality, it's the joke of the millennium. I stand with the rest of them on the crowded floor below the TV screens. As trains are announced parts of the crowd tear loose and rush for their track. I think of Ina, how she has a really nice voice. Voices are intriguing, especially those that don't yet have a physical body attached to them. I wish I could date just a voice, select the love of my life only with the help of my ears. Then inside me it would bloom and come to life. I guess this is how blind people live, but they do still have smell and taste and touch, it's never just the voice. But I don't want it telephoned, I want it floating next to me all the time. I can't stand being on the phone for hours, although with Ina I was. Easy talkers have me wary after the Kate incident, but Ina felt slightly different. Different as in the little differences that make the ball fall either on the left side of the court or the right. There's no skill involved, just the odd portion of chance. A new line appears on the TV screen, and another part of the herd cuts loose and scurries away across the floor. New members quickly fill in from behind, and soon the number of people staring at the screen is back to the same. Homeostasis. The world is always striving to revert back to balance.

I spot her across the hall. It's funny how there are certain people you can spot in a crowd. They light up as if made of phosphorus because your biology combines in a favorable way. Nobody else can see it; only you can see who your biological body matches. I know it's pseudoscience; it's not even science, only a game. I play it at times when I spot a girl and I think what it would be like if we were to live the rest of our lives together. What I'm saying is that sometimes I look at girls wearing my what-if glasses, and looking through them today I see a glowing phosphorus being standing out from all the rest. At once my brain attaches itself to her and fast-forwards well into our relationship. My brain must be truly desperate, the way it longs for the story of life to become the reality of life. But this time I do agree with my brain and see no reason to chastise it. She is a Belle-Belle, a striking nymph, and when the number of my train track finally pops up on the screen I hope and resolve, at the same time, that if we are going on the same train I will talk to her.

I let chance do half the work; the rest I chip in. The stalking only takes me as far as sitting on the other side of the walkway, with her one row ahead of me. Then, when she slips out her iPod, I emerge from the shadows and seize the moment. Something about "trading music" is my opening line, although I don't see it as such. It's simply how the moment presents itself, and I run with it. Her name is Beth – a lovely name as far as names go, and the name of a song, but I don't say as much, even though together we enter the kingdom of music through the gate of bands with animal names. We both agree that bands with animal names have made a comeback. In the sixties there were of course the Beatles, the Animals, the Monkees, the Byrds, and so on, but just off the top of our heads, and from our iPod playlists, we count off as many as we can of the new generation: the Fleet Foxes, Arctic Monkeys, Animal Collective, Gorillaz, Modest Mouse, Atomic Kitten, They Shoot Horses, Don't They?, Panda Bear, Counting

Crows, Snoop Dogg, Pussycat Dolls, Dinosaur Jr., Bloodhound
Gang, Sparklehorse, and Moby. We debate for a while whether
Moby is considered an animal, and we finally decide, as the train
rears to a stop somewhere in New Jersey, that although a fictional
character he counts as a whale. I find out that Beth is short for
Bethany and I think it's great because only young girls should
have short names, and the two go together like cheese and peas.
She is wearing a yellow dress that, although it looks faded in the
sun, has the swelling texture of fabric dipped in saltwater. I expect
it to crackle as she moves, but it doesn't make a sound. As a whole
Beth is a colorific enigma. Her eyes are green-pitted mirrors of
innocence, her hair is a reddish-brown nuance of burnt clay, and
her skin is white as an Englishman's. I consider this as the train
alternatively stops and moves forward. I watch Beth's lips move as
she speaks, we hand our iPods back and forth, playing animal song
after animal song, and on this train chugging through New Jersey
marshland, something that I haven't realized until now suddenly
becomes clear to me. I have a list.

What I mean by that is that when I look at Beth's lips I
discover that I am truly attracted to a certain shape and form of
lips. Beth's lips are exquisite. The perfectly vaulted upper arches
that meet in a slumped *V* and the straight but fleshy lower lip
could very well have been made out of wax. They look so new
and symmetrical that for a moment I doubt their authenticity. It
has never occurred to me that I am one of those who have a list,
but as of today I already have two things to put on it: a certain
voice and specifically shaped lips. Beth's stop is coming up and
as she struggles with the plastic covering a new stack of business
cards I stow the list away for the time being. I think that if I keep
my eyes open and complete it, perhaps I can break down a woman
into miniscule pieces, detail by detail, and when I'm done I will

reassemble her in the world. Once I know her composition I will seek out the perfect one.

I spend the night at Ina's. Not because she's the one, but because NYC Transit and Ina want me to. She makes roasted chicken and with it we have red wine while we talk about the contents of her bookshelf just across the room. Afterward she tries teaching me the salsa, or perhaps it is the samba, I'm not sure. Whatever dance it is, it doesn't go great. Ina has an electric cigarette and when I first pick it up I figure it is only a ceramic sculpture, a reminiscence of the nineties, but then she "lights" it when we are laying naked across the tussled bed sheets, and I am truly astonished by the vapor trickling out from one end. Moments later, locked in the bathroom, I close my eyes and silently wish there was a way I could appear in my own bathroom. Ever since childhood I have at times experienced this acute longing for home when stranded in strange places. Once, when I was a around 12, my mother had to pick me up from my friend's cabin simply because the longing had hit me so hard that it had suddenly caused my tear ducts to overflow. But I'm a grown-up now and the maternal rescue force has been permanently put on hold. Instead I open my eyes, and without shedding one single tear I get back in bed and will myself to sleep. In the morning, while Ina wrestles with her outfits and general appearance, I get a chance to examine the electric cigarette more closely. I knew it was a trick all along.

We walk through a neighborhood where families live like families do, past not-yet-opened corner stores, to arrive at a bus stop outside a boarded-up Borders. Suited and trenchcoated men and women get on at several stops before we finally dip into the cool of the tunnel and swim under the water, back to the real world. We part on the subway. Below a poster of monstrously magnified bedbugs we do the whole kiss-hug-cha-cha-cha, while in my right side pocket I am fingering Beth's business card and the electric cigarette simultaneously. After Ina is gone the bedbugs and I continue on, and after a few more stops she is almost completely erased from my mind. nd I know this is the reason – the fact that I have developed the ability to forget someone so quickly – that I feel so vacuous.

It's Friday. Diane must have the day off, for she ignores my messages. I don't see Bri either and that comes as a great relief when I log in and see that I have a message from her in my profile inbox. I know what it says before I even read it – meaning, once I read it I know I could have guessed what it said without opening it. Her response is exactly what I had predicted. If there was a department in the FBI that did profiling for online dating, I could probably manage it. Or at least be their star agent. The Dating Agent. And with Bri, since I was the one who wrote her profile in the first place, it's almost too easy. With 80 percent of messages sent by males going unanswered, you need to understand a few things to get in bed with the statistics. There are a number of things one can do to lure that first reply from women online. And once you have the first reply chances double that you will get a second. In fact, for every reply you get, the chances that you will get another double again, until you are sitting across from her, sipping another fucking café latte.

If I really had been at the FBI, right now I would have pulled out one of those large presentation pads on a stand, and on it I would have scribbled with my black felt pen, in front of a small but highly motivated crowd dressed in white shirts, black pants, and black-framed glasses, the Bureau's most finely tuned minds.

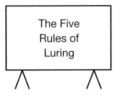

The Five
Rules of
Luring

NUMBER ONE – START WITH A JOKE

"Hello, I'm a serial killer just let out of prison" or "You+Me +Vegas=Wedding?" These are both good examples of messages that are funny but not over the top, that stand out against the imbecile flood of Hellos and What-up-mamas. Nine of ten women say that humor is a turn-on. But it's a balancing act in which it's easy to step over the line. Just remember, when the party is over, nobody wants to go home with the clown.

NUMBER TWO – COMMENT ON HER PROFILE

It's there for a reason, and you can show her that you are at least interested enough in her that you read her profile. Comment on what she does for a living, where she's traveled, or a quirky detail, like the fact that she is deathly afraid of chipmunks. If you are interested in someone, chances are they will be interested in you. That's the first herpes of dating, the second comes later. If you are lucky.

NUMBER THREE – COMMENT ON HER PICTURES

She may be wearing a nice dress or riding an ATV across the sand dunes in Pismo Beach. Pictures are easy to comment on or ask questions about. But don't just say the obvious, like, "So, I see you've been to Paris." "Duh, no I pasted the Eiffel Tower into an old photo, then took a photo of it before I posted the whole thing in an attempt to scam the French." And don't let your first comment be about sex, rape fantasies, killing, or serial killing (unless you are implementing Number One).

NUMBER FOUR – SEE THROUGH HER

People talk a lot of shit, and when someone can see through that shit it is impressive. Even if it's your own shit. That makes them real, thus, in turn, making *you* real. And despite the fact that society at large is trying to escape reality as much as possible, reality is and always will be there when we come down from our TV methadone highs.

NUMBER FIVE – EVERYBODY IS LOOKING FOR LOVE

This is the reason we are here, and I'm not just talking about online dating. Everybody is looking for the piece that fits the hole. Let her know you know that, that you have named Love your guiding star, and you will instantly become a man of substance. Sometimes a man of substance can even get away with being ugly.

Class dismissed.

When I was young, younger than a whippersnapper but older than a tot, catalogue women were the subject of many a fantasy. It's Saturday, and I find an old Sears catalogue from the late seventies at a garage sale in Williamsburg. I'd rather not be here in Hipster Town, where there are more scruffy beards, ripped jeans and flannel shirts than in Lumberjack City, Canada. If hipsters were a species they would be catalogued somewhere between bedbugs and the ants that eat your house from the inside, if you ask me. The garage sale is only a few blocks from Bedford, but it's mostly crap, except for the Sears catalogue that I buy in a jiffy. But I'm not in Williamsburg for the garage sale, and it's not for the brunch nor for the secondhand shops that now outnumber the firsthand shops, nor for the organic bakeries or ever-emerging art galleries. I'm on my way to the old Domino Sugar Factory. It was once the world's largest sugar refinery, built by the Havemeyer family in the 1880s. But all history aside – and there must be plenty to tell of the rise and fall of the building with the neon sign that looms over the East River like a beacon – I go there for one reason specifically: the sugar stalactites.

It's a behemoth of a building that springs from the ground as one enters from either of the streets running west–east from the water. A million old bricks stacked on top of each other on Kent Avenue, between South Fifth and South Second Streets. Like a castle from the past that has become too expensive to care for, it is in poor shape, with many broken windows – the ones along the ground floors boarded – and, judging by the amount of droppings on the sidewalk, home to at least half of Brooklyn's pigeon population. Although, despite her size, there's something playful about her, like a toy house that you can open up in the middle to look inside each tiny room. But there's no denying it, she is a hulking beaut, as far as buildings go.

The streets all around the block are empty and deserted, and the whole compound is enshrouded in a netted fence. But I know where to go. Just where the website stated, on the north side, there is a hole cut big enough for a person to squeeze through, and when I reach the water I find the blue door at once. I feel like the gummy bear version of Indiana Jones as I locate the stairwell in the gloomy lack of electric light, and although some illumination would have helped, it turns out I don't need my eyes as much as I need my nose to know where I'm going. The sugar factory is a microcosmos in itself, a miniature Hawaii with different climate zones for each elevation. On the first floor there's an earthy smell: dark, damp and heavy. I move carefully up the stairs, and the air becomes somewhat lighter and the smell is sharp, almost acrid. On the third floor the aroma is musky, and a breeze moves through the building; on the fourth it is the same, but lighter. First on the fifth do I encounter what I've been looking for, the seductive sacchariferous odor tumbles against me, and that's how I know I'm right.

The fifth floor contains of a big hall that most likely continues into other halls and rooms, but I dare not walk around for fear of falling through some hidden crack in the floor. Besides, I've only come for the stalactites. I find them almost in the middle of the first hall, hanging down from the ceiling. They resemble something from the Stone Age – not stone, although they do have the same texture and color, but rather ancient spears. They cling to the old pipes that run in large rectangles above me, and it's as amazing as anything I've ever seen. Very fine, powdered sugar that has mixed with droplets of water for years and years, until fossilized. I wipe one off with my sleeve (it still looks dirty) and stick the tip of my tongue to it. It's amazing. The sweetness that spreads though my mouth, and all around my body, reverts me straight back to childhood – the sugar acts as the plutonium for the flux capacitor: it gives me wings, and when I land I am right back in the eighties. I'm between ten and thirteen and I am in my room, wearing a pajamas, flipping through my mother's mail-order catalogue. The women pose with headbands that don't do much to hold their fuzzy hair down, wearing colorful, patterned jumpsuits, and for the first time I feel something I have never before. I look at the pictures – it started out as an innocent exploration of a glossy magazine, but with each page I flip past I, unknowingly, inch one step closer to becoming a man. One by one the women come alive, and they begin churning the little blood I have within, and without knowing how it happened, I am hard. It's a puny penis, hairless, but it stands like a spring twig under my pajama pants. Wanting to be nearer to them, to feel and touch, I lean in close and I put my lips on the pages, and that's enough for it to happen. Without knowing it I have entered onto the long and winding road leading to manhood, and from that point on there was no turning back. The catalogue women, like enchanted nymphets, became forever embedded in my mind, and little did I know that for every day that passed, more and more of my thoughts would revolve around them. I remove my tongue from the aged sugar phallus and feel the catalogue pulsate in my back pocket. I wonder where they are now, all those women from all those catalogues. Some are probably dead, others married and living in San Antonio, but I like to think of them as eternally catalogued. I don't want the sugar factory to decay, and I don't want the women who guided me into my manhood to become sugar stalactites of memory.

EIGHTH CHAPTER

Monday morning, and Diane is back. She's my only real friend at work. With the others, the physical ones, I keep pretty much to myself. Not that I shun anyone, but I have this aversion to speaking to people who know exactly what I do all day, and vice versa. We would only look down on each other simply because we know how utterly useless the things we do are. Diane is the exception, and as strange as it may sound, I think perhaps that's because we have never met and perhaps never will. It's a silent pact between us, to never drag this loathly embarrassment out into the open, where it will surely putrefy and infuse us with disgust for each other. We keep it to our rectangular callouts, and without having to talk about it, I know Diane feels the same way.

Used panty
vending machines
in Japan is a myth.

It's sort of amazing, but not entirely, that our link-leaping has taken us both to Japan. I don't know exactly which way she took to get there, but as it is, Diane has acquired special insight into the huge but often vastly underestimated dirty-old-Asian-man market.

What I find out, through square bits of information, is that Japan has the highest number of vending machines per capita, with about one machine for every twenty-three people. Diane tells me about some of the more unusual kinds. The egg-vending machine in which each compartment contains a bag of eggs. The eggs come from a nearby farm, and the farmer has to fill the machine daily. The umbrella-vending machines are there for whenever the rain decides to come down on your parade – if you have coins, that is. One of my favorites is the necktie-vending machine. Picture being on your way to the most important meeting of your life, and you happen to catch a glimpse of your reflection in a window. You forgot to put on a tie this morning! Necktie-vending machine to the rescue! Although you still have to tie it yourself. The live lobster–vending machine allows Japanese gamers to try their hand at catching live lobsters, arcade style. The rice-vending machine is of course a big hit in Japan, as seems to be the case with the toilet paper–vending machines. But I'm not entirely sure about the fresh vegetable–vending machine.

What is lacking, in my opinion, on the otherwise completely developed Japanese vending-machine market, are a couple of obvious niches. One day I would really like to see a vending machine that sold other vending machines, preferably those stacked with virgin Japanese schoolgirls with tentacle vaginas. I'd save all my coins. But right now, I tell Diane, I'd settle for one that sold sumo wrestlers.

SUMO

Sumo a competitive full-contact sport from Japan where a wrestler (*rikishi*) attempts to force another wrestler out of a circular ring (*dohyō*) or to touch the ground with anything other than the soles of the feet. Matches often last only a few seconds.

A sumo wrestler leads a highly regimented way of life. On entering sumo, they are expected to grow their hair long to form a topknot, or *chonmage*, similar to the samurai hairstyles of the Edo Period. Furthermore they are expected to wear the *chonmage* and traditional Japanese dress when in public. Consequently, sumo wrestlers can be identified immediately when in public.

Rikishi are not normally allowed to eat breakfast and are expected to have a form of siesta after a large lunch. The most common type of lunch served is the traditional "sumo meal" of *chankonabe* which consists of a simmering stew cooked at table which contains various fish, meat, and vegetables. It is usually eaten with rice and washed down with beer. This regimen of no breakfast and a large lunch followed by a sleep helps *rikishi* put on weight so as to compete more effectively.

The negative effects of the sumo lifestyle become dangerously apparent later in life. Sumo wrestlers have a life expectancy of between 60 and 65, more than 10 years shorter than the average Japanese male. They often develop diabetes, high blood pressure, and are prone to **heart attacks.**

HEART ATTACK

Myocardial infarction (MI) or acute myocardial infarction (AMI), commonly known as a heart attack, is the interruption of blood supply to a part of the heart, causing heart cells to die.

Classical symptoms of acute myocardial infarction include sudden chest pain (typically radiating to the left arm or left side of the neck), shortness of breath, nausea, vomiting, palpitations, sweating, and anxiety (often described as a sense of impending doom).

Heart attacks are the leading cause of death for both men and women worldwide. There is an association of an increased incidence of a heart attack in the morning hours, more specifically around 9 a.m.

At common law, a myocardial infarction is generally a disease, but may sometimes be an injury. This has implications for no-fault insurance schemes such as workers' compensation. A heart attack is generally not covered; however, it may be a work-related injury if it results, for example, from unusual emotional stress or unusual exertion

Immediate treatment for suspected acute myocardial infarction includes oxygen, aspirin, and sublingual **nitroglycerin**.

NITROGLYCERIN

Glyceryl trinitrate (GTN) is an alternative name for the chemical nitroglycerin, which has been used to treat angina and heart failure since at least 1870. Despite this, the mechanism of nitric oxide (NO) generation from GTN and the metabolic consequences of this bioactivation are still not entirely understood.

It is often recommended that GTN transdermal patches should be removed before defibrillation due to the risk of explosion, but careful investigations have concluded that reports of apparent GTN patch explosions during defibrillation are in fact due to voltage breakdown involving the metal mesh in some patches.

It has been questioned whether GTN patches do indeed combust or explode when exposed to the energy from a defibrillator. It has been proposed that this is in fact a myth. According to the *MythBusters* television show this is the case and GTN patches do not explode.

A recent medical development will include a small amount of nitroglycerin in the tip of a new Durex **condom** to stimulate erection during intercourse.

CONDOM

A condom is a barrier device most commonly used during sexual intercourse to reduce the probability of pregnancy and spreading sexually transmitted diseases (STDs – such as gonorrhea, syphilis, and HIV). It is put on a man's erect penis and physically blocks ejaculated semen from entering the body of a sexual partner.

... According to a study in the Sexually Transmitted Diseases Journal of the American Sexually Transmitted Diseases Association condoms have a breakage rate of 2.3% and a slippage rate of 1.3% which "may translate into a high risk for individuals who are very sexually active." With proper knowledge and application technique – and use at every act of intercourse – women whose partners use male condoms experience a 2% per-year pregnancy rate with perfect use and a 15% per-year pregnancy rate with typical use.

Condoms have been used for at least 400 years. Despite some opposition, the condom market grew rapidly. In the 18th century, condoms were available in a variety of qualities and sizes, made from either linen treated with chemicals, or "skin" (bladder or intestine softened by treatment with sulfur and lye). In 1839, Charles Goodyear discovered a way of processing natural rubber, which is too stiff when cold and too soft when warm, in such a way as to make it elastic. This proved to have advantages for the manufacture of condoms; unlike the **sheeps'** gut condoms, they could stretch and did not tear quickly when used.

SHEEP

Sheep (*Ovis aries*) are quadrupedal, ruminant mammals typically kept as livestock. Like all ruminants, sheep are members of the order Artiodactyla, the even-toed ungulates. Although the name "sheep" applies to many species in the genus *Ovis*, in everyday usage it almost always refers to *Ovis aries*. Numbering a little over one billion, domestic sheep are also the most numerous species of sheep.

A sheep's wool is the most widely used animal fiber.

Sheep have horizontal slit-shaped pupils, possessing excellent peripheral vision; with visual fields of approximately 270° to 320°, sheep can see behind themselves without turning their heads.

A minority of sheep display a preference for homosexuality (8% on average) or are freemartins (female animals that are behaviorally masculine and lack functioning ovaries).

Sheep and goats are closely related as both are in the subfamily Caprinae. However, they are separate species, so hybrids rarely occur, and are always infertile. A hybrid of a ewe and a buck (a male goat) is called a sheep-goat hybrid (only a single such animal has been confirmed), and is not to be confused with the genetic chimera called a **geep**.

GEEP

A sheep–goat chimera (sometimes called a geep in popular media is a chimera produced by combining the embryos of a goat and a sheep; the resulting animal has cells of both sheep and goat origin. A sheep-goat chimera should not be confused with a sheep-goat hybrid, which can result when a goat mates with a sheep.

The first sheep-goat chimeras were created by researchers at the Institute of Animal Physiology in Cambridge, England by combining sheep embryos with goat embryos. They reported their results in 1984. The successful chimeras were a mosaic of goat and sheep tissue. The parts that grew from the sheep embryo were woolly. Those that grew from the goat embryo were **hairy.**

HAIR

Hair is a filamentous biomaterial, that grows from follicles found in the dermis. Found exclusively in mammals, hair is one of the defining characteristics of the mammalian class.

Many subcultures have hairstyles which may indicate an unofficial membership. Many hippies, metalheads, and Indian sadhus have long hair. Many punks wear a hairstyle known as a Mohawk or other spiked and dyed hairstyles; skinheads have short-cropped or completely shaved heads. **Mullet** hairstyles stereotypically have been associated with rednecks.

MULLET

The mullet is a hairstyle that is short at the front and sides, and long in the back. Often ridiculed as a lowbrow and unappealing hairstyle, the mullet began to appear in popular media in the 1960s and 1970s but did not become generally well-known until the early 1980s. It continued to be popular until the mid-1990s.

According to the Oxford English Dictionary, the term *mullet* was "apparently coined, and certainly popularized, by U.S. hip-hop group the Beastie Boys", who used "mullet" and "mullet head" as epithets in their 1994 song "Mullet Head".

In Canada, the northern United States and Sweden, the hairstyle is sometimes known as "hockey hair" or "hockey player haircut", as it was common among their ice hockey players in the 1980s.

Punk rock band The Vandals sang of country music singers and **Jerry Springer Show** guests sporting mullets, and listed regional names for the style in the 1998 song "I've Got an Ape Drape".

THE JERRY SPRINGER SHOW

The Jerry Springer Show is ostensibly a talk show where troubled or dysfunctional families come to discuss their problems before a studio audience so that the audience or host can offer suggestions on what can be done to resolve their situations. The show has come to epitomize the so-called "trash TV talk show", as each episode of the show focuses on topics such as adultery, zoophilia, divorce, homophobia, incest, infidelity, pedophilia, pornography, prostitution, racism, strange fetishes, dwarfism, or **transvestism**, which frequently result in fighting between guests.

It's six on a Monday evening, and I am standing outside Serendipity, wondering if her tits are fake. I know the lights are on: they are hard to miss, the way they bulge out, I'm just not sure anybody's home. Her name is Kelly, and on her profile she had one demand: the man she sought was not to have any tummy fat. She was, however, the beautiful, dark-skinned, fine-limbed, and symmetrically feline-faced Amazon I had many times pictured myself being with, so I laid my aversion for stupidity aside, at least for the moment. That is also the reason I let myself be cajoled to East 60ᵗʰ Street for dinner and not a simple meet-and-greet at the coffee shop across the street from work. Stupidity, or my weakness in the face of desire.

We sit under Tiffany lampshades, a bit slow on the draw. She is reserved on the outside, courteous, and rather hard to gauge. I get the feeling she comes from a background much different from the one we are sitting in right now. She's left the poorer quarters, and now it troubles her that it might flash through her seams, so she keeps her head low and waits for me to make a move. I order a Salmon a la Garden of Allah, she takes a Bi-Sensual Burger. She finishes off with a Chocolate Blackout shake, but not before I bluntly stumble across the racial fence, threatening to tear the whole damned thing down. I start by asking about black women. My curiosity is innocently teeming within, but I'm not sure I can even say "black," so first I ask her. For a moment I think I have made a grave mistake. But it turns out the tension was only a piece of Bi-Burger stuck behind a front tooth. I exhale and merrily continue down the road spiked with blunders. My second question is a reply to her question about my favorite food. I name a few things then turn it back to her. I say chicken because it's what comes to mind. I'm sure I don't say fried chicken. She freezes up again and I trace my words back, and only after a while do I get it. We continue and talk about hair. I refuse to believe it's common knowledge that black people have special hair. They can't wash it every other day because it's fuzzy. Upon hearing this I reach out to touch it and she slaps my hand away, not maliciously, it's only a reflex, for I see that a smile has begun to glow under her mask. "Never touch a black woman's hair," she says, and I add that to the list, right after chicken, of things not to say or do. Talking to her is a field of verbal mines that go off all around me the further I continue. And although her appearance has softened when she sucks her Chocolate Blackout shake through a thick straw, I thank my lucky star that I am an immigrant. It has worked against me many times, in banks for example, or any place where they keep dumb clerks behind a desk, but here it is the one thing that graciously carries me out of the battlefield without a scratch.

When we are done I pay the bill – this is another thing I put on the list: black girls don't go dutch – then we head east, past Dylan's Candy Bar, and enter a furniture store. It's nearly eight and only a few minutes to closing. We browse the living-room section one floor down, viewing a few couches, and while we do I try to locate the bubble of love where I should discover that time stands still. But it's vehemently lost. All I can think of is that I want to go home. It's the first time, I realize, I've felt post-sex withdrawal without even having sex. Finally she picks a couch. It's a grey piece the size of a yellow cab, with black double stitches flurrying across it like skid marks. We sit with straight backs next to each other. When I feel the weight shift I know she is leaning towards me, so I turn, and we kiss, and at that very moment the store speakers announce that it's closing time. There's really only one more thing I want to know about her, then we could part forever. I want to know about her boobs. She sees that there is something on my mind and urges me on, not with words but with her facial expression. In a panic I revert back to the minefield and pick the first thing that comes to mind. I ask her why it's not called Native Africans, like Native Americans, but just as she is about to answer a security guard steps down the stairs, and we get up, leave the store and split up clean on the street outside. I can only stand and watch the mystery of the probable fake boobs disappear unsolved down the sidewalk.

It's Tuesday, and I'm back at the FBI. It's the case of Bri, and we are trying to crack it by profiling. Two things happen: I have a reply from her in my souped-up profile inbox, and I have a message from her on the screen. At first I think the message on the screen is from Diane, but once I read it, all becomes clear. Even as I go to her office my confidence is at an all-time high. Most likely I'm suffering from delusion and steadily on my way to going crazy, next stop the funny farm, but the whole idea of flirting with disaster gets me high. I can't see how she can have anything on me. And I am right, she doesn't. But she does ask some circling questions about her profile, if I've heard anything, if all is normal, and I say yes, no, I haven't heard anything, everything is normal. Then I walk back to my desk feeling like one of the guys from *Ocean's Eleven* after emptying the vault. Right then and there, I take out my pad and on it, in front of the entire group of rookie agents, I continue my lesson.

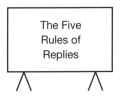

The Five
Rules of
Replies

NUMBER ONE – BE POSITIVE

Always be positive. Be a lover, not a hater, and all that jazz. She says nails through the eyes are fun, you say I'll bring a hammer. Everyone loves a yea-sayer, and positivity is truly contagious.

NUMBER TWO – KEEP IT SHORT

Don't overwhelm with the story of your life. Pick a reply that is short but sweet, one that sticks to her medulla oblongata like ham on rye.

NUMBER THREE – HOLD YOUR HORSES

Don't suggest that you meet in the first reply. It stinks either of desperation or doubtful intentions, neither of which is a good cologne for you to be wearing. You have already shown your interest by replying; leave the rest open and exciting. Nobody can refuse a good riddle.

NUMBER FOUR – TURN ON A DIME

Show another side of yourself, an unexpected one. Opposites are always intriguing. A model who is also a wrestler or a bodyguard who folds origami makes for a more interesting combo than an investment banker who lives near Wall Street, enjoys wine and sudoku, and plays squash in between bouts of raping the stock market.

NUMBER FIVE – SUBLIMINAL MESSAGES

Just like playing "Stairway to Heaven" backwards, think lovey-dovey when you write your reply. Somehow – and Led Zeppelin can attest to this – it will show through. Perhaps it's that the words arrange themselves in such a way that they strike a chord in the reader, perhaps it's something else. Either way, you have nothing to lose, and it just might give you an edge.

I congratulate myself on being a smooth smoothie but decide to hold off on replying a second time. I obviously don't want to date Bri. Besides, she would fire me the instant she finds out. If I'm honest, I really don't want to date anyone. Occupational hazard, I guess, just like a chef. When he comes home, the furthest thing on his mind is cooking a hearty meal. I bet you, of all the people in the world, nobody eats more crackers and slumgullion than chefs. But what can I do? I just can't cut myself loose.

I don't have any crackers, and I thank god that I don't have any slumgullion, but there's something about the day, something almost ominous that makes me decide that I have do something about my life. I work in a place that melts my brain, I date women I don't want to see again, and I am generally displeased with my life. I wish I could blame someone – the communists, the vegans, anybody – it would be so much easier. To have a front against which I could unite my anger. But everything is so fucking politically incorrect these days, there's nobody to blame. Not even the dying polar bears. But I have made up my mind. I will make a change. Michael Jackson said it, so why can't I do it? "It's gonna feel real good, gonna make a difference. Gonna make it right…".

Come to think of it, I realize that I really have everything I need to start. I have time, for one, even here at work, and I have thoughts. If I could implement one with the other, it could make for a… change. I could start some sort of business. Though the problem is, I don't really want to make anything or sell anything that has to be made, so that right there pretty much restricts me. I decide to start with the next best thing to an actual idea, and that is opening an Excel document. It is the most business-suited program I have on my computer and I'm confident it will do the job. For a long time I stare at the empty cells, trying to coax out of them a lucrative vision. I'm jamming with the Excel document, hoping something will pop. By lunchtime nothing has, and I decide to give it a rest. Then, from out of nowhere – the elevator must have jarred something loose again – when I come back I have two great ideas, just like that. Producing nothing, selling nothing produced, equals an online business. The first one I call Shitter.

Shitter – sharing your most private thoughts

In the infinite universe, great thoughts have coalesced in one place more than any other: the toilet.

The toilet seat is a veritable greenhouse for the brain. Breakthrough inventions, literature highlights, strategies for ruling nations, multibillion-dollar business ideas, love poems – they all have the inspiring privacy of the toilet to thank. So the next time you find yourself on one with a moment to reflect, join the great ones – share your thoughts with your friends, and with the world.

Shitter – there's no place quite as inspiring.

I write it down. However, the Excel document proves to be most unsuitable for my undertaking. The cells are too small, and even though they expand to fit the text, when I move on to the next cell the text in the first cell is hidden. But I do like the way the columns are symmetrically stacked, so I use it anyway. My first idea seems good for a little while, but once I have it all written down it occurs to me it is about as useless as Michael Jackson's doctor. Instead, my second idea, e-publishing, presents itself as a great option. I try to find a unique selling point for my particular e-book business, and I come to think about when I was young and went to the used-book store to read comic books. I could stand there for hours and flip through pages that smelled of kids' sweaty hands and Kool-Aid. From there the idea comes to me on big, flapping wings. I'll sell used e-books! I'll create a marketplace where people sell their old downloads at the fraction of the original price, except there are no tears on any pages, no coffee-mug stains and no pubic hairs nestled between pages 12 and 13. I like the idea so much that I fill up cell after cell until my document begins to resemble a chessboard. It's new, it's fresh, and it will be a punk-rock zap to the publishing industry. I can't see any weak points until it occurs to me: the torn pages, the coffee-mug stains – although not the pubic hairs – those are all things we *want* from a secondhand book. The scent of history, that's where the value of secondhand things lies. Easy come, easy go. I try for a while to pull forth a third splendid idea, but I seem to momentarily have depleted my mind of gold. Instead I move on to books.

Books are a touchy subject. The first one I wrote ended with a lawsuit and a dead icon. Perhaps I should write about that, call it *A Lawsuit and a Death*. It would be similar to *Four Weddings and a Funeral,* except it wouldn't have any funny parts in it. Bad idea. Perhaps I should write a book about bad ideas? Animal bondage, Kama Sutra for kids, all the opposites of cheese and peas. I try hard for a while to crap out a bestseller synopsis, but my mind has become numb and I have to stop. I shake off the sudden lash of ambition and use the little energy I have left to slug out ads for the company until it's time to go home.

It's on the subway, a couple of hours later, that it comes to me. Perhaps it's because of the rocking – it mimics the movement of the elevator, only laterally – or perhaps it's the residue of my earlier brainstorm. Either way, I get a great idea for a book. The reason I come to think of it, besides the rocking, is sitting across from me, dangling his legs from the seat while thoughtfully stroking his moustache. His head is abnormally large, or so it seems. It's really that the rest of him is grossly underproportioned – puny, to be frank. I turn my head from side to side and glance at him every time I pass. The dwarf is a marvel of nature that I hate to leave when my stop comes up, but I hurry home to put pen to paper and don't stop until I have the whole project outlined. Finally.

Later that same evening the energy from my new idea still buzzes inside my head. There's a real hullaballoo in there. Had I only known it was this easy to change my life, by simply putting a mental foot down and deciding, I would have done it a long time ago. Little by little the hullaballo simmers down to silence, and I fall asleep, wildly content.

What I need is to get away from the office for a few days, and I have a plan. They seem to come to me with ease these days. Two quarts of heavy cream loom ominously next to my screen, waiting to do their part in my rueful scheme. I could have just called in sick, but the impact is so much greater when it is physical. The stain will be skipped and hobbled over for days, and each time anyone, including first and foremost Bri, does that little jump of controlled disgust, thoughts will go out to me. But first I have to get some things together. Primo numero uno, my secret self needs to get back to Bri. Then, although reluctantly, I need to line up a new date for my real self. I have realized that, despite my brief fallout yesterday, it comes down to simple math: there are a certain number of women circling in my universe, and in order to find The One I must go through as many as possible. Finally, I want to get back to Diane about my latest link-leaping update. I notice with a spiteful glee that none of the things on my agenda are work-related except messaging Diane, sort of. So while the morality is ambivalent, I start on my reply to Bri. As I do, I figure I might as well also get started on the cream, so I take a swig and down it goes without problem. It's easy for me to keep the right emotional distance. I am correct and moderately charming, yet slightly curt. When I read my own reply, imagining I read it for the first time, I think of myself as an independent man, capable of being generous with his emotions, but until unlocked, slightly distant. All in all, it's a trustworthy and honestly painted picture. I send it off, my unknowingly illicit spawn that stands no chance of blossoming.

Before my second task I take another swig of cream, emptying the first carton halfway. Choosing a date, is that what it's come to? No different than buying a car. I choose Kana for one reason only, and that is her sign-off. Every message she ends with something combining animals and sex, such as "Japanese pussycat" or "Japanese naughty snake" or "Japanese yummy lion," and even though neither personality test nor star signs combine in our favor, her sign-offs are enough for me. When I'm done with the Japanese pussycat, the first carton of cream is also done. I tap Diane on her electronic shoulder, and she responds right away. She ended last on a serial killer in Poughkeepsie, and considering the way we stray further and further from our original departure, I am beginning to doubt we will ever make our way back. I open the second carton of cream and begin from the *Jerry Springer Show*.

TRANSVESTISM

Transvestism (also called transvestitism) is the practice of cross-dressing, which is wearing clothing traditionally associated with the opposite sex. When cross-dressing occurs for erotic purposes over a period of at least six months and when it causes significant distress or impairment, the behavior is considered a mental disorder in the Diagnostic and Statistical Manual of Mental Disorders called transvestic fetishism.

See also

– I Am My Own Wife

I AM MY OWN WIFE

I Am My Own Wife is a play by Doug Wright based on his conversations with German transvestite **Charlotte von Mahlsdorf.**

CHARLOTTE VON MAHLSDORF

Charlotte von Mahlsdorf was born Lothar Berfelde, the son of Max Berfelde and Gretchen Gaupp in Berlin-Mahlsdorf, Germany. At a very young age she felt more like a girl, and expressed more interest in the clothing and articles of little girls. In her younger years she helped a second-hand goods dealer clear out the apartments of deported Jews and sometimes kept items for herself.

Max Berfelde, Lothar's father, was already a member of the Nazi Party by the late 1920s and he had become a party leader in Mahlsdorf. In 1942 he forced Lothar to join the Hitler Youth. They often quarrelled, but the situation escalated in 1944 when Lothar's mother left the family during the evacuation. Max demanded Lothar choose between her parents and threatened her with a gun. Shaken by this, Lothar struck her father dead with a rolling pin while he slept. In January 1945, after several weeks in a psychiatric institution, Lothar was sentenced by a court in Berlin to four years detention as an anti-social juvenile delinquent.

With the fall of the Third Reich, Lothar was released. She worked as a second-hand goods dealer and dressed in a more feminine way. "Lothar" became "Lottchen". She loved older men and became a well-known figure in the city as von Mahlsdorf. She began collecting household items, thus saving historical everyday items from bombed-out houses. Her collection evolved into the Gründerzeit Museum (a museum of every-day items). She was also able to take advantage of the clearance of the households of people who left for **West Germany.**

WEST GERMANY

West Germany (German: Westdeutschland) is the common English name for the Federal Republic of Germany or FRG (German: Bundesrepublik Deutschland) in the period between its creation in May 1949 to German reunification on 3 October 1990.

From the late 1950s onwards, West Germany had one of the strongest economies in the world, making among other things the **Volkswagen Beetle**, for many years the most successful car in the world.

VOLKSWAGEN BEETLE

The Volkswagen Type 1, widely known as the Volkswagen Beetle and Volkswagen Bug, is an economy car produced by the German auto maker Volkswagen (VW) from 1938 until 2003. With over 21 million manufactured in an air-cooled, rear-engined, rear-wheel drive configuration, the Beetle is the longest-running and most-manufactured automobile of a single design platform anywhere in the world.

In 1933, Adolf Hitler gave the order to Ferdinand Porsche to develop a Volkswagen (literally, "people's car" in German. Hitler required a basic vehicle capable of transporting two adults and three children at 100 km/h (62 mph).

Mass production of civilian VW automobiles did not start until post-war occupation. Opinion in the United States was not flattering, however, perhaps because of the characteristic differences between the American and European car markets. Henry Ford II once described the car as "a little box." The Ford company was offered the entire VW works after the war for free. Ford's right-hand man **Ernest Breech** was asked what he thought, and told Henry II, "What we're being offered here, Mr. Ford, isn't worth a damn!"

ERNEST BREECH

Ernest R. Breech (1897 – 1978) was an American corporate executive. Although he is best remembered for his work in revitalizing Ford Motor Company in the years following World War II, he served similar roles at Trans World Airlines and other companies.

At Ford, before the so-called "**Whiz Kids**" came on the scene, it was Breech who cleared the ground for expansion by trimming away Ford's corporate fat.

WHIZ KIDS

The Whiz Kids were ten United States Army Air Forces veterans of World War II who became Ford Motor Company executives in 1946.

They were led by their commanding officer, Charles B. "Tex" Thornton. The others were:

Wilbur Andreson – left after two years to return to California and became an executive with Bekins Van Lines.

Charles Bosworth, retired as director of purchasing.

J. Edward Lundy, retired as chief financial officer – he remained at Ford through the 1970s and was known as one of the most powerful people in the company and as a confidant of Henry Ford II.

Robert S. McNamara, who eventually became the president of Ford. He then became the Secretary of Defense and the President of the World Bank.

Arjay Miller, rose through finance and became Ford president in the mid 1960s. After being dismissed in favor of Bunkie Knudsen, an executive recruited from General Motors, he became the dean of the Stanford Business School.

Ben Mills, became general manager of Lincoln-Mercury Division.

George Moore, left after two years to become an automobile dealer.

Francis "Jack" Reith, became head of Ford of France and was a rising star. Subsequently he was the executive responsible for the Mercury Turnpike Cruiser and heavily involved in the Edsel, both sales failures. Reith left the company to run the Crosley Division of Avco, and committed **suicide** a few years later.

SUICIDE

Suicide (Latin *suicidium*, from *sui caedere*, "to kill oneself") is the act of a human being intentionally causing his or her own death.

Over one million people commit suicide every year. It is a leading cause of death among teenagers and adults under 35. There are an estimated 10 to 20 million non-fatal attempted suicides every year worldwide.

In a study conducted among nurses, those smoking between 1-24 cigarettes per day had twice the suicide risk; 25 cigarettes or more, 4 times the suicide risk, than those who had never smoked.

Near the end of WWII the Japanese designed a small aircraft whose only purpose was kamikaze missions. The Japanese also built one-man "human torpedo" suicide submarines called **Kaitens**.

KAITENS

The Kaiten (Japanese: 回天, literal translation: "Return to the sky", commonly rendered as: "The turn toward heaven", "The Heaven Shaker" or "Change the World" were manned torpedos and suicide craft, they were used by the Imperial Japanese Navy in the final stages of World War II.

The very first kaiten was nothing much more than a type 93 torpedo engine compartment attached to a cylinder that would become the pilot's chamber and trimming ballast in place of the warhead and other electronics and hydraulics. The torpedo's pneumatic gyroscope was replaced by an electric model and controls were linked up to give the pilot full control over the weapon.

The original designers and testers of this new weapon were Lieutenant Hiroshi Kuroki and Lieutenant Sekio Nishina. They were both to die at the controls of kaitens, Lieutenant Kuroki being in a very early training prototype.

Early designs allowed the pilot to escape after the final acceleration toward the target. There is no record of any pilot attempting to escape or intending to do so and this provision was dropped from later kaitens so that, once inside, the pilot could not let himself out. The kaiten was fitted with a control for self destruction, intended for use if an attack failed or the impact fuse failed.

American losses accredited to kaiten attacks came to a total of 187 officers and men, the losses of kaiten crews and support staff are much higher. In total 106 kaiten pilots who lost their lives (including 15 killed in training accidents and 2 suicides after the war). In addition to the pilots, 846 men died as eight Japanese submarines carrying kaiten were sunk and 156 maintenance and support personnel were also killed.

The tradition of death instead of defeat, capture, and perceived shame was deeply entrenched in Japanese military culture. It was one of the primary traditions in the samurai life and the **Bushido** code: loyalty and honor until death.

I only get to kaitens before a white cascade of cream erupts from my insides. I have enough presence to turn away from my computer, but I never make it out into the corridor. Instead my milky vomit ends up covering every inch of my office floor. It's really a razzmatazz of crapulence. My head spins and I breathe rapidly, strings of white hanging from my open mouth. *I'm a loser*, I think, but I can't help but smile. For this, regardless of my failing aim, will land me the rest of the week off.

I start as soon as I get home. I find my old Systematic camera in the last box I take down from the top shelf of the closet. Stowage of old memories. If one were to chronicle the life of such boxes, it would be a tale of being moved from apartment to apartment to house to retirement holding room to storage and eventually to the top closet shelves in children's apartments, from where it goes round in a circle again. Stuff we lug around when we are young we lug around for the rest of our lives. Those weights make us a little bit slower and a little bit more reluctant to move with every year that passes. What was it Tyler Durden said in *Fight Club*? "The things you own end up owning you." It's a pathetic source of life wisdoms, but sometimes life is just that.

I start putting the boxes back. They contain books, high school journals, photos, trinkets, one stuffed woodpecker on a stick, a deflated football, letters from a time when letters came on paper, stickers, notebooks: an assortment of worldly crap valuable to only one person in the world. An image of the closets in my apartment building enters my mind, then one of all the houses in my neighborhood, then the entire city, then the entire country, finally the world, all of them crammed tight with boxes filled with crap. I decide to break the link right now. I get a roll of black garbage bags from the kitchen; the boxes are enough to fill three. I look out my window and see them sitting on the curb, and it's peculiar, seeing part of yourself from afar like that. Like floating above your body as you die. Tyler Durden was right; I do feel lighter now, more free.

I leave for the city with my camera, but it turns out my spot-and-shoot plan was a bit optimistic. There simply aren't enough dwarfs walking around the streets of New York City. When I get back, the hunter without his catch, I revert to the one place one can find anything, even dwarfs, I hope – the all-containing online garbage dump of the world – Craigslist. I'll make the dwarfs come to me instead.

With this last one there are now lots of ads in my life; I realize it as I wait for Kana outside the juice bar. She arrives, in disarray, before I can figure out what impact that will have. I say disarray because her outfit seems to be in shambles, but I soon learn that this is just the way she dresses. I couldn't describe it in detail, for I know not where to begin, other than saying that many things protrude at many a strange angle, employing feathers, metal, and leather. We go to a bar in the West Village, and I have to sit at arm's length from her so as not to be speared by her outfit. I don't comment upon it and neither does she, and the further the night progresses, the greater becomes my insight into her insanity. But I don't care much about that. What bothers me mostly has nothing to do with her. What suddenly itches worse than crumbled crackers in bed is the form modern dating has taken. You meet, you talk to get to know each other, meaning that one person provides color while the other person the canvas, and then you switch places and the other person paints, until two crude images, dripping wet, are left outside some bar only to be washed away by morning. Dating is an endless repetition of who you are, what you do, and where you've been. To get something from it, to not feel robbed and empty when you walk away, you need to inject something turbulent into the conversation every now and then. Something that sets things on end. But with Kana's outfit and her lisping Japlish, her references even in the spoken word to animal creatures and sex, I excuse myself and sneak out without saying goodbye. At least my painting is still largely uncreated.

Human life is a sham. Why is it that nobody has blown the whistle on it? Why isn't life exposed in the world's news as a fraud? Where are the carbon-footprint-obsessed environmentalists shouting their lungs out for the sake of a life that isn't delivering? It's late morning, and I wake up all moist from a sweaty dream and instantly feel depressed because waking up doesn't make me happy to be back in the real world, only sad. I refuse to get up. I'm a slugabed, and at random I pick up a magazine from the floor. I aimlessly flip it open, and my eyes land on the life cycle of the tent caterpillar. The tent caterpillar leads a life straight as an arrow, genetically programmed from Day One until death amongst moss. The adult moths lay eggs on a cherry-tree twig in July − for some reason only cherry will do − and they do not hatch until the following April or May, during which they must withstand freezing blizzards and dehydrating sun and wind. Hatching time coincides with the appearance of the green leaves on which the minute caterpillars feed. Every evening hundreds of them proceed down to the first crotch of the tree, building there a web in which to spend the night. They continue eating during the day, then crawling down to the web to sleep, all through May. The caterpillars are slugabeds too. So, when finally they are fully grown they crawl down the trunk of the tree one last time, find a shelter, and there spin about themselves a silken cocoon. Within this cocoon the caterpillar changes into a chrysalis with wings, long legs, antennas, and the various structures of the moth. This takes about two weeks. The moth can fly, but it no longer has a digestive system; its only remaining appetite is a sexual urge, and it hides out all day and flies around all night in search of a mate. This is its only mission in life and the sole reason for its former life stages. The male, after mating, dies. The female first finds another cherry tree, where she plants her fertilized eggs, before she dies too.

I wish our lives were as self-contained. Then there would be no need for dreams, desire, fear, or frustration. Just one, two, three, and back in the ever-evolving circle of life. Our only impulse, our single mission in life, would be to roam the streets at night, with great big hard-ons or moistened holes, trying to find a mate. Reading about the tent caterpillar cheers me up somewhat. It's not just the article's description of the nightly sex missions that does it, it's really because of the cocoon.

It's been a long time since I imagined myself in one. I used to do it all the time when I was younger. Back then I could be afraid for no reason, I still can; it's a dread that creeps up on me, and suddenly the whole world seems dangerous. My neighbor, people on the street, eight-year-old kids. Now I can deal with it, but back then the cocoon was my only protection, if only an imaginary one. The cocoon was a pod of unbreakable glass or plastic in which I laid snug on my back, sometimes looking out, sometimes completely hidden by a velvet curtain. The cocoon was unbreakable, unshakable, always protecting me against everything. While I was in it nothing could happen to me. I could be pushed over a steep cliff, but the pod would only bounce down and land safely at the bottom, holding me in comfort inside with cushions of air. The pod could be plunged into the ocean, but not a drop of water would penetrate the seamless structure, and the air would never run out. It could be put on stage in front of a thousand people, and although all thousand would laugh and stare and point their fingers, the pod would drape itself in velvet and keep me safe and warm inside. I could be in a pit ten feet deep and filled with snakes, but even watching them cover every inch in front my face wouldn't scare me inside my chamber. Inside my pod I would be safe from all fears, from danger, from everything bad the world could ever produce.

But then one day I had a dream about it and everything changed. I was in Africa, on the savanna, and bloodthirsty lions were circling the pod, pounding and pushing at it with their great dirty paws. When they tried to bite through the transparent surface I could see into their throats, past their pinkish tongues, all the way into the darkness of their bellies, but not a scratch could they make on my pod. Finally they gave up, and I watched them as one watches lions at the zoo, comfortably, from a safe distance

. . . until I saw Teresa. Teresa was my girlfriend at the time, and why she came walking across the savanna I don't know, but when the lions saw her they charged and tore her to pieces. That's the day I discovered that although the pod could protect me from all fears, all danger, and everything bad the world could ever produce, it couldn't protect me from heartache. I was fifteen at the time, and the next day Teresa broke up with me. But worse than that, one of the greatest losses of my life, was the annihilation of my cocoon. It had become a kaiten, and I could never feel completely safe in it again.

NINTH CHAPTER

I have a message from three dwarfs this morning; I suppose it's the equivalent of 1.5 whole replies. I clear out part of my living room, scoot the couch to one end of the room, and string up a white sheet over the window to keep the light out: wham-bang, I have created a makeshift photo studio. It looks like a badly arranged porno set, and with my first visitor standing in front of the sheet, straining his lips in a ridiculous grimace, I'd say it could very well be. He's the strong, silent type, doesn't say much or even ask me about the project, and if it wasn't for his aberrantly staring eyes I would have been more relaxed. Instead I'm tense and mess up the first photos, and when I finally get my act together I run out of film. I look all around my apartment for a new roll but realize I must have thrown it out with the boxes of collected past. It's only luck that the bags still sit on the sidewalk. I hurry down to scavenge through them while a silent dwarf with crazy eyes is posing in my living-room corner. After that the rest of the shoot goes smooth as a Ken Doll.

I decide to use him from the feet. The next guy doesn't show until after lunch and he is, if possible, an even bigger weirdo. Are all dwarfs freaks? The questions begs an answer as a miniature Elvis wobbles into my apartment. In the white Vegas outfit studded with rhinestones, complete with cape and a cloud of heavy cologne, the little fellow bobs back and forth so much I'm not sure I'm getting any sharp pictures. And all while humming the same old tune, over and over, as if Elvis only did one song with a hook good enough to remember. I shoot a few more for good measure, his lips curled in a silent snarl, and I decide to only use him from the feet up as well.

The third one arrives shortly afterward and he is, to my utter surprise, totally normal. His name is Frank, and he is a piano player. Every night, except Sundays and Mondays, he plays the piano at a bar named Short Stop over in Greenpoint. After I've shot my takes I offer him a beer. I've always had a lot of respect for musicians, how they string together a living from nothing, and we talk for a little while. He doesn't mind being short; it's who he is, and he figures he's gotten more women the way he is than if he'd been of normal height. It's a good point, and I decide to use him from the face down, not just because he seems to be a nice guy, but because his face is expressive in a sad sort of way, with his things-I've-seen-in-bars eyes. We talk about the project, and Frank says it sounds like a project alright, and that I should come by Short Stop if I need more pictures. It's a little people–adjusted bar, where everything is miniature, and I say that that sounds really cool, and Frank shrugs his shoulders and says yeah, but without much conviction. When he's gone I feel good and pretty good at the same time. Good for having started my project, and pretty good because that's how I feel when I picture myself in a miniature bar.

There's so much sex in the world that sometimes I can't think of anything else. Once I tried to count all the number of times I thought about sex in one day, but I ended it when I realized that my method was deeply flawed. I needed to remind myself to remember, so I wrote SEX in big black letters on the back of my hand, but every time I saw it I thought of sex. Anyway, all in all, I think it's well over ten times a day, but it could also be over a hundred. It could be the littlest things, a dog's asshole for example. If I walk behind the lady with a bulldog, before I can pass her I've gotten a good glimpse of her dog's asshole, and with this picture my mind will devilishly conjure up an image about sex. The bad part is that it's not limited only to bulldogs' assholes. Sometimes just seeing an old lady will do it. It's pretty disgusting. I'll be the first one to admit it; men are animals, but I can't help it. Mostly however, thank the lord, I think of sex when I see pretty girls. But it's a real sickness to be plagued by, and I suppose a lot of people are affected by it. Perhaps not all are as badly affected, but I'm sure there is sufficient damage done to promote some serious research in this field alone. For instance, what if I reduced my sex thoughts by half and instead used that space to ponder useful things? I could solve problems I didn't even realize existed, I could learn new things that would benefit the world, I could do charity work or any number of useful things with the time currently occupied with the thought of diving into the other sex.

I don't really picture myself diving into a pussy, but I do like to frolic within the area of one. Anyway, once again, useless sex is on my mind as I enter Short Stop. It's around nine and I hear the tunes from a piano through the door. Upon entering I quickly discover that the only thing that's full-sized is, in fact, the piano. Frank looks awfully small where he sits behind it, and whenever he plays the furthest keys he has to lean so much to the side that I think he will fall off the stool. I take a seat at the bar – correction, I tower over the bar, with the short stool padding the backs of my knees. It's a positive surprise to find that the beer glasses are also full-sized, but much of everything else is shrunken, as if tumble-dried at too high a temperature. All around me little people do what people in bars do normally. Nobody pays me much attention, even though I am a giant in the land of Lilliput, and I think I have Frank to thank for that. A woman comes up to me. I look down and wonder how I must come across. She climbs up on the stool next to me, and I nod at the barkeep for another beer. It turns out Frank has told her about the project, and while we get to know each other I can't help but revert back to the bulldog's asshole. Gloria is her name and her lips are painted red and shine glossy from below, covering and uncovering a set of sharp, carnivorous teeth. It's not long before she invites herself back to my place, and as we ride in the back of a cab I can't help but feel I am doing something wrong. I come to my own rescue; although vertically challenged, dwarfs aren't children and they aren't mentally handicapped – she is a grown woman who can decide for herself who she rides in a taxi cab with. Not even five minutes after we get to my place, just enough time for me to take a piss and step out from the bathroom, she takes her independence to another level. I find her standing in front of the strung sheet, completely naked. Her body has that dwarfy muscly quality, stocky and compact, but she is oddly well-proportioned in her own peculiar way. It is like nipping the corners of a picture in Photoshop, drawing it towards the center so that everything bundles up slightly, each limb gaining a swelling roundness. She urges me to photograph her, and with trembling fingers I navigate the camera with a clumsiness that would have made a grade schooler feel superior. I notice she hasn't got any hair between her legs. It's the epidemic of the twenty-first-century, the little-girl complex responsible for uprooting uncountable rugs around the world. In all fairness I have to cut her some slack: she really is a little girl, except for her eyes, which play seductively my way. But all the rest — shaved vaginas, smooth boxes, bald kitties, and barren vulvas — what in the bygone times of pop culture ever caused the largest human defoliation in the history of mankind?

I snap picture after picture, and when I run out of film I put the camera down and for a moment we stand face-to-face, both aware of what is about to happen. I wonder about size. What about her size? I think about babies being squeezed out of openings the size of apricots, and I gather nature always finds a way. We move closer, and I'm just about to put my hands on her shoulders when there's a knock on the door. I leave her standing by the window, uncovered, to go see about the door. I try to look through the hole but it's so dirty I couldn't even have spotted an elephant through it, and I swing the door open. Suddenly something explodes behind the hinges. The next thing I know, some fast-moving deity hammers my ball sack with a penetrating biff as it bursts into the apartment. "Oh, Jimmy…" I hear Gloria's voice from where I lie holding my nuts in the hallway. Soon the two of them pass above me, which in my misty state I think must be nice for a change, and without a word they leave. I have no choice but to stay where I am until my balls have gone from a thundering pain to a less acute and steady throbbing, and despite it all I manage a smile. It's just another night in zooville.

Despite my contempt for Corporate A, I feel like a traitor when I put foot in an office when I'm supposed to be home sick. But the feeling quickly passes as I think about my speech. It's about having the guts to be original, someone who stands out from the flock. Obviously I use animals to convey my picture clearly. The man and woman opposite me are publishers. I tell them that they can choose from three things: they can be the sheep, the wolf, or the herder. If they are part of the flock of sheep they are like everyone else in the group, but everything seems frightening because they know the wolf can lurk around any corner. The wolf doesn't really exist; he is just a vivid figment of the imagination that embodies all the wrongs. The herder is the individual, the one who sees the herd from a distance and the world in perspective. I tell them all this even before I get to the book because I know that a good hook is vital, and I see on their faces that they are, although slightly perplexed, mostly intrigued. And that's when I lay it on them. My idea.

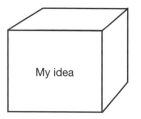

The BIG Book about Little People. I show them the pictures, except the ones of Gloria, how they only show from the feet up to the neck, or from the head to the knees, while the book itself acts like a cropping board, cutting everything that doesn't fit the paper. A book with life-sized photos of dwarfs is the perfect coffee-table book, because A) it doesn't exist, B) dwarfs are both mysterious and politically correct, and C) the art world has always been in favor of dwarfism. I see that they are shaken, they don't say a word, and then the weirdest thing happens. Sitting there, with the project gutted before me, I suddenly think it is a completely shit idea. Only after I've taken a step back am I able to see it. Without giving it another thought, like a junkie seeing the smack train roll in, I excuse myself and dive out of the office. Leaving the photos and everything, out I go. Back home, I try to forget all about crummy business ideas, dwarfs, and most of all books, which is what got me in trouble to begin with.

Correction: it wasn't trouble to begin with, it only got me there later. I wrote it, and she was my muse and my spell-check. I met her at a party, on a rooftop in Williamsburg of all places, and it wasn't long before she moved in with me. Like everything, it started with fun, both her and the book, and then one day they both turned on me. Just like that.

Was her name Vicky? No, it wasn't. Was it Bertha? No, it wasn't. Well, what was her name then? I'm not saying. There, there John David – you don't mind me calling you that, do you? That's my name. Do you miss her? Is that a fair assessment? Assess my ass. There, there John David, let's not use such profanities. Let's try to be curt. Choke on my penis shaft, numbnuts. There, there. Let's start from the beginning. Where did the you two lovebirds meet? Was it a clear day in April, a warm day in June, or a chilly day in September? Was it... I've told you, I met her at a party on a rooftop in Williamsburg. Now get off my back you flimsy make-believe psychologist!

The L train to Bedford, when it dips from Avenue C into the underground, going deep to avoid the strident water of the East River, howls like an animal. For a second it feels as if we are set loose: rails no longer apply and we all go thundering into the unknown, ears popping, spines shaking. Then we hit a slight rise and it's over. We skid into the Bedford stop, and when the doors open all the demon hipsters of the world swarm the platform and disappear howling up the stairs and into the night.

She might have been on that very same train. Only later did it occur to me. She might have brushed past me, flung her hair in my face, banged her knee into mine without knowing that two strings tied to our respective waists led up to that rooftop. Faith was pulling us along, tossing us unseen clues to the future, block by block.

I was supposed to meet Gustaf there: the rooftop thing was hosted by a friend of a friend of his. Gustaf has curly blond hair and, more often than not, thick black-rimmed glasses. He cuts a sharp image, every inch of his face meticulously sculpted, but that evening he was nowhere to be seen. Music played; I heard it from the street below, and in the elevator it echoed metallically through the shaft. A girl from Argentina or Brazil or maybe Uruguay hiked her pants up a few feet from me and applied lipstick without the help of a mirror. She wore a top hat and kept mumbling something in Spanish, like she was giving herself a pep talk.

When the doors open the music wells into us, and as if sensing its force, we both lean forward, taking a strident stand against the wave of incoming Cs and Gs. I lose her there, the Argentinian girl who might have been Brazilian or even Uruguayan, and I keep my eyes out for Gustaf. It's not easy to find anyone, for the roof is filled with bodies. I walk aimlessly under a pencil-gray sky, around clusters of kids, half hoping to spot my friend, half hoping not to so that I can leave early. Tiki torches run in glowing candy-colored bubbles along the short end of the roof, and I am drawn towards them. I am a single moth working my way towards the light, both literally and metaphorically, without even knowing it. At roof's end, between a yellow ball and a red ball of light, I take a seat on the ledge. Despite the crowd around me, I feel lonely and detached from it all, as if I am floating in the air ten feet above, just watching. I am absorbed to such degree that I shudder when I feel the hand on my arm. I think for a moment that I will fall off the edge and down to the unforgiving pavement below, but as the tingle subsides I steady myself. She sits in the next gap, nestled softly between the yellow and a green, and she keeps her face directed my way. Her hand hangs motionless in the air. Freeze the moment. Many times after I have wondered, if I could have, would I have? Kept everything where it was, the party on the roof, the music like a steady wall in the background, no dips, no silent moments, just a steady beat – would I have frozen time if I could? The sky continuously penciled darker and darker, but no matter how long we sat there it would never reach total blackness. Only different shades of grey. The torches forever alight, creating small, luminous clouds of warmth that blend perfectly with the cooler evening air. And in the midst of all that beauty you'd find us: sitting on the rooftop ledge, my left side colored red, my right side yellow, attaching perfectly to her left-side yellow. I'd have this startled look upon my face, but one not plastered there by fear or any of his cousins. Instead it was a face of awakening and seeing for the first time the truth. Truth's hand would hang in the air, lifeless, yet very much alive. It would have been the perfect rendition of a modern classic, life as depicted on countless church ceilings. The big bang captured at the precise moment of detonation.

She moves into my heart and my apartment the same week. Neither caused any trouble. Even her boxes seemed light. Circumstances had it so, and who were we to argue? She's a blogger now, one of those coffee mug–carrying fashionistas who gets free makeup in her daily mail. For a while I not only scanned her blog, I devoured every word of it, bloodhound searching for any references to me. The heartache she felt, the pain, the tears, the longing. But all I found was brain-mushy raving about the latest collection from Yohji Yamamoto.

I stopped some time ago, reading it. The mundanity of it made me physically sick. Coffee and clothes, dogs the size of squirrels. Ironically, it used to be the other way. I was the one writing, and she was the one wagging her tail with excitement. Those were happy days. The bed was always only three feet away, never made, and a constant jumble of soft and cool. Every day was a Sunday, and my apartment was a universe. It was like we had reverted back to the magical world of childhood, only with adult perks. The borders of our world were narrow: the food store one block over to the west, the park and the East River one block to the east. At the center were my apartment, my notebooks, my laptop, and the bed. A kingdom of cotton, paper, and love. But no matter what anyone tells you, love never lasts forever.

TENTH CHAPTER

I'm back at work, cleaned, cleansed and refocused. A little hiatus does the body and mind good, they say, and perhaps that's what I'm feeling. I logon and see that I have a message waiting from Diane, and I must say she surprises me.

> How are you?

This is the most personal she's ever been, but I don't have time to digest it for just then Bri summons me to her office. She asks me if I'm feeling better, then onward we go through some business structure questions, before she cuts to the chase. Could I take a peek behind the scenes for her? Sure, I say and take the paper she hands me and drift back to my rectangle.

I'll deal with Bri's request later; now it's friendship time. Diane has dropped the bomb, and I return it in all its shy splendor.

Fine.
How are you?

It's a cascade of heartwarming words between two souls deeply connected. But then... I must say, despite my careful trot into the stadium of companions, I expected more of Diane. I spied an opening, a crack in the otherwise watertight wall that has kept us on an anonymous level of friendship, below friendship even, I dare say. I really thought now was the time for us to cut our hands, mix our blood, and spit in the air. I was looking forward to getting to know her: Diane, the woman behind the rectangle. It's no great mystery what she does all day, but what does she look like, where does she live, what does she like to eat, what are all the similar trivialities that defines her? Where does she fit in in the human food pyramid?

Speaking of food, I imagine she's fat. I should really have no grounds for thinking it, but, however slightly, several details points to it. First of all, it's the way she types. It's not just the way she types but more so what she types. Or the way she types what it is she types. It's always short, almost curt, and although that could be due to the structure of our internal messaging system, it is precisely the preciseness and the perceived speed that gives her messages a certain zing. The zing leads to my conclusion that she punches the letters in with her fat fingers, fast and precise, as if making a statement. I control this. I don't control my fat body but I can make my fat fingers dance like a wiry ballerina on this keyboard, and by God, if I can't have the other at least that is where I will be agile. Secondly, people who are different, those considered fat, fish-eyed or platypus-nosed, most often have developed, as a defense against the ruthless world, a shield of thoughts that deflect its meanness. This shield makes other people jerks, and machines instead become their brethren. Machines don't talk back, they don't laugh at you, they don't whisper behind your back and don't not invite you to a party— machines are emotional equalizers. They don't care who you are and what you look like; as long as you want to use them they'll come crawling up into your lap for a good scratch. Fat people like machines for this very reason, not because they're lazy, but because machines are the only true friends in a cruel world, and with a little practice—perhaps it's not even about practice, but a gift—one can learn to see the signs of this friendship. I see it in Diane's messages, the way the machine almost helps them along, and delivers them swiftly without any static resonation. This is my theory, and I was delighted when I saw the message from Diane this morning, as it presented a gateway into my guesstimates. So naturally my disappointment was great when all I got from my hopeful attempt was

I'm on Solomon Shereshevsky.

I google him, and what I find out shocks me – not to the core, but it reverberates within me as the damnedest riff. Solomon was the man who remembered everything. Born in Russia in 1886, he had a memory so perfect that he could vividly recall every single minute of his life, even from when he was a baby. His talent was discovered when he worked as a newspaper journalist in Moscow and his editor noticed that Solomon never took any notes during meetings. When he confronted his employee he realized that Solomon could remember everything the editor had ever said, at every meeting. Subjected to many tests – for example, memorizing complex mathematical formulas and huge matrices – it was revealed that Solomon wasn't actually smarter than anyone else. In fact, he didn't score very high on IQ tests. But his ability to remember everything was phenomenal. The reason for this, concluded starry-eyed Russian scientists with huge moustaches, was that when Solomon heard or saw something he also experienced its taste, its sound, its smell, and its structure. He didn't make it happen, it was just something that happened automatically. One person's voice might sound to Solomon crumbly and yellow; another looked like a flame with fibers protruding from it. Once Solomon refused to buy ice cream from a woman because he experienced her voice as black cinders bursting out of her mouth.

I vividly recall my ex's voice as snakelike curls of rusty razor-sharp wire when she said she wanted to take a break. The whole room folded into itself, leaving only darkness, but darkness on an angle – although I didn't see anything, I sensed everything was on an angle. And the smell, Jean Paul Gaultier, that wasn't a miracle at all. It was simply her perfume. I don't know where it went wrong, for me or for Solomon, but it did go wrong. Somewhere we strayed from the road onto a path that led to the house of the wicked witch. Solomon lived his life mainly in his thoughts and memory – they were less confusing than the world. He ended up as sort of a touring freak show, Solomon the Mnemonic, and neither cured cancer nor laid the basis for constructing an eternal source of energy. I am the man who remembers only certain parts of his life, but those parts haunt and confuse me just as much. I hope I don't end up in a freak show, but I doubt anyone would pay money to see me talk about my ex-girlfriend.

I try to numb my faulty memory by racking up another date. I snatch her from the pond of information, or in my case disinformation, and we decide to meet later that evening.

I meet Adele at the border of Soho, Chinatown, and the Lower East Side in a Manhattan no man's land, a thin strip of cobblestoned street that seems to have fallen between the cracks of real estate. For this quality of authenticity, this slice of universe served up, I approach her with a hugger-mugger of a whisper. "Hey," and right away I realize how much of a creep I sound like, a comic-book-reading, still-living-with-his-mom creep, and I quickly raise my voice several decibels, "I'm John David," – *and I just hit puberty* is what I want to add, but I don't.

Within fifty steps I find out the following: Adele's parents are from Mexico, she once sang with Ricky Martin (to which I exclaim, "He's gay!"), she works at Nike as an assistant something, and she has a beautiful face, a rather zaftig body, and a voice smooth and strong like a jazz chanteuse's. She is sort of hesitant about meeting someone from online, I can tell, but in a curiously charming way, and when we pass a place that has a patio and I ask her if she wants a drink, she says, "Sure, but keep your hands to yourself, buddy," as if someone had told her this was when guys like me made their move. But I don't, nor have I planned to move anything.

It's a Caribbean place, coconuts and parasols, but no reggae. I'm suddenly very thirsty, on the verge of dehydrated thirsty, so I order a lemonade. Adele has one too, and we talk about the details, but it is still nice. She is agreeable and we get along swell, and as the hours pass her laughter becomes infused with a peculiar island ring and the lemonades have made way to breezers and coolers. When the bar closes and I have found no fault in her and she no fault in me, I suggest we grab something to eat. "Come along," she says, "I know a place," and she drags me off – in a cab, but still it feels as if I am fastened to her and wherever she goes, I must follow.

Consequently we end up in a diner on 34th and 8th. It is one of those old-style places where the atmosphere breathes history and movies of another time, but you never know these days whether the place itself is old or if it's only the carpentry. Anyway, Adele seems to know her way around the menu and racks up a sizable order from the poor waitress, who scribbles it down as fast as she can, and I don't want to be half the man, or even half the woman, so I tag along. There's something serene yet exciting about all-night diners. Serene because the sharp light, white as a flash against the dark surroundings, cuts each wrinkle, each pale face and tired slouching back, into razor-sharp images, and exciting because these are the hours when everybody else is asleep. We are living on nonexistent time, we are urban explorers or vampires, and if we are just a little bit lucky we will see what the sleepers never will. You snooze, you lose, and you don't get any bacon and pancakes or scrambled-egg fajitas either.

Eventually the food arrives on huge, steaming plates, and while Adele tells me about piñatas, how in Mexico there are special stores for them, *piñaterias*, and why she would never have sex with anyone on the first date, I stuff my face with food and think about sex. I think the food brings it out in us, in her especially, the passion. The passion for food is essentially the same as sexual passion: we have but one desire, and it flares up in different stadiums. I think that the food she eats, the massive amounts set before us, work just as well as any kisses, caresses, and whispers.

When we are done and I feel the end credits start rolling, she, after much deliberating, flings herself into my cab, and without further ado we ride like zonked-out cholesterol junkies to my house. "Only sleeping," she says as we both get into bed, and again she explains, not about the piñatas, but how on a first date she could never do it. The room is spinning somewhat, the lipids, taking us to a not uncomfortable high, and when we turn the lights out and lie in bed, pretending to be two corpses, it only takes a minute before we are fucking. Then we sleep, and in the morning we fuck again, so much that my penis begins to bleed. It's the chafing, the coarse black Mexican pubic hair that Adele keeps cropped but not shaved, and the pointy follicles brush against me with every stroke and eventually a tiny drop of blood forms at the base of my shaft, my skin rubbed thin and then pricked by an especially sharp fang. Adele then helps herself to a hearty breakfast, or at least that's what it sounds like with pots slamming and cabinets banging, and I lie in bed with my eyes closed and pretend, just for a second, that this is my life every morning, that the slamming and banging is an everyday occurrence before we both rush off to work, me and my Amiga. But when the greasy stench of something frying finds its way into the bedroom, I snap out of it and suddenly feel sick to my stomach.

We part at the subway station, and I feel as if the car taking me to work rocks more than usual. It's either a fat hangover – I didn't know about them before – or it's just a symptom of my chafed cock. I decide it's the former, for when I pass a hot dog vendor the smell of the juices makes me want to vomit, but when I pass a gorgeous girl in a beige business suit, delicate and stern, neither I nor my cock objects even the slightest.

At work everything at my desk looks the same. It always does. Time ceases to exist when I leave my rectangular prism.

I've already decided to forgive Diane for yesterday's ice-coldness. Now that I think of it, it's really fine the way things are. We are link-leaping buddies, two toilet books befriending each other, and we should leave it at that. I begin to wind up the old engine, but before I can even look at any of the ads I have to crank out I pick up the leaping right where I left off.

BUSHIDO

Bushidō (武士道?), meaning "Way of the Warrior", is a Japanese code of conduct and a way of the samurai life, loosely analogous to the concept of chivalry. It originates from the samurai moral code and stresses frugality, loyalty, martial arts mastery, and honor unto death. Born of two main influences, the violent existence of the samurai was tempered by the wisdom and serenity of Japanese Shinto and **Buddhism**.

BUDDHISM

Buddhism is a religion and philosophy encompassing a variety of traditions, beliefs and practices, largely based on teachings attributed to Siddhartha Gautama, commonly known as the Buddha (Pāli/Sanskrit "the awakened one"). The Buddha lived and taught in the northeastern Indian subcontinent some time between the 6th and 4th centuries BCE. He is recognized by Buddhists as an awakened or enlightened teacher who shared his insights to help sentient beings end suffering (or *dukkha*), achieve nirvana, and escape what is seen as a cycle of suffering and rebirth.

According to the Pali Tipitaka and the Āgamas of other early Buddhist schools, the Four Noble Truths were the first teaching of Gautama Buddha after attaining Nirvana. They are sometimes considered to contain the essence of the Buddha's teachings:

Life as we know it ultimately is or leads to suffering/uneasiness (*dukkha*) in one way or another.

Suffering is caused by craving. This is often expressed as a deluded clinging to a certain sense of existence, to selfhood, or to the things or phenomena that we consider the cause of happiness or unhappiness. Craving also has its negative aspect, i.e. one craves that a certain state of affairs not exist.

Suffering ends when craving ends. This is achieved by eliminating delusion, thereby reaching a liberated state of Enlightenment (*bodhi*);

Reaching this liberated state is achieved by following the path laid out by the Buddha.

This method is described by early Western scholars, and taught as an introduction to Buddhism by some contemporary Mahayana teachers (for example, the **Dalai Lama**).

DALAI LAMA

The 14th Dalai Lama (religious name: Tenzin Gyatso, shortened from Jetsun Jamphel Ngawang Lobsang Yeshe Tenzin Gyatso, born Lhamo Dondrub, 6 July 1935) is the 14th and current Dalai Lama. Dalai Lamas are the most influential figures in the Gelugpa lineage of Tibetan Buddhism, although the 14th has consolidated control over the other lineages in recent years. He won the Nobel Peace Prize in 1989, and is also well known for his lifelong advocacy for Tibetans inside and outside Tibet.

Tibetans traditionally believe him to be the reincarnation of his predecessors and a manifestation of the Bodhisattva of Compassion.

Regarding the killing of Osama bin Laden, the Dalai Lama said, "Forgiveness doesn't mean forget what happened ... If something is serious and it is necessary to take counter-measures, you have to take counter-measures."

One South African official publicly criticized the Dalai Lama's politics and lamented a taboo on criticism of him, saying "To say anything against the Dalai Lama is, in some quarters, equivalent to trying to shoot **Bambi**".

BAMBI

Bambi, a young roe deer, is the main character in Felix Salten's *Bambi, A Life in the Woods* and in the Disney films based on the book. Bambi has starred in two movies, *Bambi* and *Bambi II*, has had cameos in several Disney cartoons, and has been parodied on occasion by other animation companies. In the Disney films his species was changed to the **white-tailed deer**, which would be more familiar to American audiences.

WHITE-TAILED DEER

The white-tailed deer (*Odocoileus virginianus*), also known as the Virginia deer or simply as the whitetail, is a medium-sized deer native to the United States (all but five of the states), Canada, Mexico, Central America, and South America as far south as Peru.

The North American male deer (also known as a buck or stag)

usually weighs 130 to 300 pounds (60 to 130 kg) but, in rare cases, bucks in excess of 375 pounds (159 kg) have been recorded. In 1926, Carl J. Lenander, Jr. took a Whitetailed buck near Tofte, MN, that was estimated at 511 pounds live weight.

Males re-grow their antlers every year. About 1 in 10,000 females also have antlers, although this is usually associated with **hermaphroditism**.

HERMAPHRODITE

In biology, a hermaphrodite is an organism that has reproductive organs normally associated with both male and female sexes.

Many taxonomic groups of animals (mostly invertebrates) do not have separate sexes. In these groups, hermaphroditism is a normal condition, enabling a form of sexual reproduction in which both partners can act as the "female" or "male". For example, the great majority of pulmonate snails, opisthobranch snails and slugs are hermaphrodites.

The word hermaphrodite entered the English lexicon in the 15th century, derived from the Greek Hermaphroditos a combination of the names of the gods Hermes (male) and Aphrodite (female). Recently, the word "**intersex**" has come into preferred usage for humans, since the word "hermaphrodite" is considered to be misleading and stigmatizing.

INTERSEX

An intersex individual may have biological characteristics of both the male and the female sexes.

Since the rise of modern medical science in Western societies, some intersex people with ambiguous external genitalia have had their genitalia surgically modified to resemble either female or male genitals. Since the advancements in surgery have made it possible for intersex conditions to be concealed, many people are not aware of how frequently intersex conditions arise in human beings or that they occur at all.

Intersex was discussed on British TV for the first time in 1966, and became a topic of interest for broadcast TV and radio in the United States and other countries from 1989. Jeffrey Eugenides' novel *Middlesex* (2002) is narrated by an intersex character who discusses the societal experience of an intersex person.

MIDDLESEX

Middlesex is a Pulitzer Prize-winning novel by Jeffrey Eugenides published in 2002. Despite slow initial sales, the book became a bestseller. Its characters and events are loosely based on the author's life and his observations of his Greek heritage. Eugenides decided to write Middlesex after he read the memoir Herculine Barbin and was unsatisfied with its discussion of an intersex's anatomy and emotions.

Primarily a Bildungsroman and family saga, the novel portrays the journey of a mutated gene through three generations of a Greek family, causing momentous changes in the protagonist's life. According to scholars, the novel's main themes are nature vs. nurture, rebirth, and the differing experiences of polar opposites – such as those found between men and women. Discussing the pursuit of the **American Dream**, it explores gender identity.

THE AMERICAN DREAM

The American Dream is a national ethos of the United States in which freedom includes a promise of the possibility of prosperity and success. In the definition of the American Dream by James Truslow Adams in 1931, "life should be better and richer and fuller for everyone, with opportunity for each according to ability or achievement" regardless of social class or circumstances of birth.

The idea of the American Dream is rooted in the United States Declaration of Independence which proclaims that **"all men are created equal"** and that they are "endowed by their Creator with certain inalienable Rights" including "Life, Liberty and the pursuit of Happiness."

"ALL MEN ARE CREATED EQUAL"

The quotation "All men are created equal" has been called an "immortal declaration", and "perhaps" the single phrase of the United States Revolutionary period with the greatest "continuing importance".

Thomas Jefferson first used the phrase in the Declaration of Independence as a rebuttal to the going political theory of the day: the Divine Right of Kings. It was thereafter quoted or incorporated into speeches by a wide array of substantial figures in American political and social life in the United States.

Jefferson may have borrowed the expression from a Polish writer and philosopher, Wawrzyniec Goslicki. Goslicki's book was part of Jefferson's **library** and was said to have influenced Jefferson.

LIBRARY

A library is a collection of sources, resources, and services, and the structure in which it is housed; it is organized for use and maintained by a public body, an institution, or a private individual.

In the more traditional sense, a library is a collection of books. Finland has the highest number of registered book borrowers per capita in the world. Over half of Finland's population are registered borrowers. In addition to providing materials, libraries also provide the services of librarians who are experts at finding and organizing information and at interpreting information needs. Libraries often provide a place of **silence** for studying.

SILENCE

Silence is the relative or total lack of audible sound.

By analogy, the word *silence* may also refer to any absence of communication, even in media other than speech. Silence is also used as total communication, in reference to non verbal communication and spiritual connection. Silence is also referred to no sounds uttered by any body in a room and or area. Silence is a very important factor in many cultural spectacles, as in rituals.

In Western cultures, it is sometimes difficult to interpret the message being sent by a person being silent (i.e. not speaking). It can mean anger, hostility, disinterest, or any number of other emotions. Because of this, people in Western cultures feel uneasy when one party is silent and will usually try their best to fill up the silence with **small talk.**

The day passes quickly, without incidents or surprises, and at four we have a staff meeting. Bri does her best to boost morale and stresses the importance of being creative, that is what will give us the edge, and when we leave we each pick whatever color stress-reliever ball we are attracted to from the bin by the door. Creative, it's the new it-word. Makes fun sound like, well… shit. Today everybody wants to be creative. I'm creative this, creative that, I don't care what I do as long as I can be creative. It's a useless tart of a goal. Hear this, all creatives. The world does not need more of your shit. So you went on a creative bender and gave birth to a couple of new T-shirt prints. So you made an app you can fuck. So you played yet another stereotyped Hollywood greenhouse-produced character designed to draw a few, although less and less, laughs in a bitingly cold darkroom. Creativity is the new religion, and like all phenomena of the masses, it develops hollow-eyed followers who live in places like Williamsburg or Venice Beach and have tattooed chests and arms, even though they've never been near a motorcycle, let alone inside a jail cell. What these copies of carbon-paper people don't realize is that wanting to be creative makes them just the opposite. Instead of saving the world with their ideas, they push their graphic designer guitar-plucking fingers through the hole of the earth and tear her apart more and more. I say hurrah for the Wall Street money monkeys: at least we all know they are evil.

Before I get off the subway I have pumped the stress reliever ball so hard that our logo has been rubbed off. I get a text from Adele. She wants to know if I want to go see a movie with her. With bacon residue still in my system I text her back, "Some other time," because quite frankly, my cock is still stinging, and for us to go to a movie and then skip the sex is not enticing enough. I might as well go alone and save myself the small talk and the holding of hands in a bucket of butter-flavored popcorn. And that is exactly what I do. I go see a movie that has lots of static camera work with desolate landscapes, shrubs, rocks, and occasionally a man with curly hair and goiterous wet eyes. The man never speaks, he only grunts, and he traverses the landscape as if searching for something or someone.

The theater is not even a quarter full, and everybody seems to have come by themselves. When I look around at the few people there, each one seemingly an isolated island, their faces take on a folorn shine from the static screen and their eyes too become bulging and their hair savage. The conclusion is that the story never reaches a conclusion. The man gets lost in the desert, and little by little he withers and finally dies on a sandy patch beneath a big boulder, his grunts the only audio backdrop. At first nobody moves; the movie has ended and the lights are on. Are we all stunned by what we've seen? Then a bald man in a polo shirt stands up in the first row and claps. Nobody joins in, and his claps complement the movie perfectly, the way they ring alone in a nearly deserted room. On my way home, if I lived in Greenpoint, I happen to pass Short Stop, and on a spontaneous notion I enter. Frank spots me right away and invites me to sit by a miniature table while he stands. "I heard about Gloria," he says, "and Jimmy." He evaluates my placid mug and finally, to connect the dots, he draws a fine red line between the two: "That kicked you in the balls." I had totally forgotten, and I look around the room as Frank laughs. "Don't worry, they're not here."

Apparently it's become quite the story at the bar, to the degree that it has even spread to other dwarf bars, perhaps out of state and maybe even as far as Germany, that Jimmy kicked a giant's ass – or, rather, balls – and all the little Davids felt mighty proud of it and wore my fall as a feather. Now, that's one place I hadn't envisioned my balls going, fastened to coat lapels and overlarge heads. But that's life for you: you never know what your ballsack holds. Frank says this sort of makes me a legend, and if a certain girl called Jenny comes to the bar, could I please pretend to be knocked out by him? He looks at me like it is only half a joke. He asks me about the book, and I answer sort of vaguely that the publishing industry is filled with people who can't tell Shakespeare from Britney Spears, that I'm waiting to hear back but don't nurture any high hopes. I just don't have the heart to tell him that I've changed my mind and that I think a life-sized book about dwarfs is the height of stupidity. *And it really is true*: the publishing industry *is filled* with college grads who studied Lord of the Rings trend analytics and crime-novel marketing while skipping the only class they should have taken, "Ideas 101: If I have Never Seen Anything Like It, It's Really Interesting." Instead assistants flood the corridors of publishing houses and agencies – everyone has an assistant, even the assistants have assistants to carry out the drearier bits of coffee-fetching, like pouring the sugar. It's an alternate universe in which each assistant has become a Russian doll: from each assistant springs another assistant, and from it another, and so on, and nobody knows what they're doing or even how to produce a good cup of coffee. Everybody is looking blindly for things already found. But I don't feel the need to be so detailed, and as I begin to worry that either ball-kicking Jimmy or Frank's infatuation Jenny will walk in any second, I suggest that we get out of there.

We walk down the street, and it feels good, like having a little brother by my side, even though Frank is probably older than me. We don't have a goal or a direction; we just walk on, and our steps sound euphonious and more real than the sound of the cars passing by, even though it's not a movie but reality, and the air is very pleasant, cool and easy, and we just walk, past burger joints, bars, sushi places, closed furniture stores, a dentist – at least I think the tall man in a trench coat is a dentist – and we let our feet do the talking. When we walk past a playground railed in by a green wrought-iron fence something suddenly goes missing: left is only the sound of my own steps. I look back and see Frank lying there on his back, twitching about, almost jumping up in the air. In a second I am by his side. I panic. He grinds his teeth and makes a terrible face. In catastrophe mode, I pull out the stress-reliever ball and shove it in between his teeth, and I hold his head so it doesn't bang against the pavement. Within a minute it's over and his body relaxes. He is covered in sweat, and he spits out the ball with a soft, wet *thup*. It bounces off his chest and rolls across the sidewalk and down into the gutter. "Are you okay?", I say. He takes a few breaths before he answers. "Epilepsy," he says. "Thanks." After a good rest we walk together back towards the bar, slow and steady, and this time all the sounds of the city are subdued. The fact that we now have a bond, that we have shared hardship, has changed something. We've almost become brothers for real. "Good idea with the ball," Frank says before we part ways. "Yeah," I say, "you have to be creative."

ELEVENTH CHAPTER

It's not how good you are, it's how good you want to be. Is that supposed to be encouraging? Is that supposed to cheer me up? I stare at the stupid letters on the fridge and feel like I am on *Candid Camera,* only not the one on TV, but the version God likes to film with one of his experiments. I want to be good. Who doesn't want to be good? But if that's all it takes, wanting, then nothing we actually do means anything. Only our intentions. And this not only makes no sense, it also depresses the shit out of me, that no matter what we do, we can't fix things. I continue to the next saying down. *Shared happiness is double happiness.* What kind of banana oil is that? Isn't shared happiness only half the happiness? If I have a chocolate bar and I share it, how can it suddenly become two chocolate bars? The way I see it, I now only have half a chocolate bar, and half the happiness.

I'd like to find the snollygoster who comes up with this drivel. There must be someone, somewhere – Jesus, Dr. Phil, or the Dalai Lama – whose sole purpose is pondering life's precious jewels, a fountain of positivity, and then transforming those soaring spiritual thoughts into simple words us mere humans can understand. I'd like to find this person and insert every little word on my fridge up his or her anus. In a moment of clarity I begin plucking the magnets off the fridge and dumping them into a box, a receptacle of keepsakes for future ass insertion. (The box does not have a label, but I can tell it apart from other boxes by the objects it holds. It contains an oyster knife so dull that I cut my hand on it, a boarding card for a Virgin flight on which a baby cried for the whole duration, an adhesive bandage that won't adhere, and a cock-flavored condom that I suspect is fake.) I've never before felt the need to get rid of them, the magnets she left behind, but suddenly it's become acute, more than a need. Actually, it's a sudden urge to cleanse myself, my soul, if you like, and I pluck down every single magnet and open drawers until I find the potato-masher doohickey and I put it all in the pirate skull bucket, and the bucket I put in the box of useless things. If I could, I would also toss in a goodly number of memories, the good ones because – and this is what I've learned the hard way – it's the good memories that hurt, not the bad ones, because what is good must turn bad, and that road only leads to disaster, but what is bad is already bad, and if it by some miracle changes it can only go up.

I would clear the whole shelf with the memory of the boat and the one with the sitcom marathon. I would clear the fridge of the messages nobody else would be able to interpret. The drive to New Jersey, the Indian birthday party, the thunderstorm and the rain that followed, they would all go in the box of things I might need but are best forgotten. I carry it out, the box with the bucket and the potato-masher dingus feels mighty heavy, and dump it on the curb next to a small mountain of trash bags. It's Saturday morning, and the entire block is sleeping in; there are no parking spaces available on the entire street, and televisions and radios are turned on and tuned in on breakfast tables where tea and toast and the Holy Ghost are devoured over telephone-book-thick newspapers. The only people out are the old, the ones who can't sleep regardless of day or who are afraid that they will never wake up if they do. I can't imagine what that would be like, going to sleep not knowing if I would ever wake up again. On the other side of the street an old man creeps forward. He looks vaguely familiar, and when he turns his face my way I see that he looks just like the Dalai Lama. The meat eating Dalai Lama. The one guy you'd expect to keep his lust in his pants, the descendant from the clouds, the chosen one, he can no longer hide the fact that he likes to chow down on a juicy burger. Where is the world headed?

I go back inside and turn on the computer. I have to get back into the game. Now that everything of her is gone, every trace erased except the flakes of skin, I have to keep going out there until the light shines in exactly the right angle on the thirteenth pillar, then the ground will rumble and the door to riches and joy will open. I'm thinking of trying a new approach. Since my current mode of choosing dates obviously isn't flawless, I will be going in the opposite direction: the opposite of whom I would normally choose to date – within certain limits of course. With ten viable candidates available, instead of choosing the one I would normally select, I will pick the one I like the least on paper. And they say ingenuity is dead. China, suck on it! Said and done, within the hour I have a date set up and I have to have done well because I'm not even excited to meet her. Everything points to an evening leading nowhere.

I'm about to link-leap when I realize it's a weekend and such frivolities should be saved for working hours only. So I sit and stare at my last link. Silence. I've never actually thought about silence before. I decide to explore it right away. It can be part of my soul-cleansing Saturday – from here on I will be a new person – and I close my eyes and try to feel it, the silence. Immediately I notice many things I usually don't notice at all. For instance, the computer is buzzing unnervingly loud. The cars driving by on the big road around the block, what an obnoxious roaring they produce! Then there's the water rushing through pipes, kids screaming, and somewhere a basketball is being bounced up and down on pavement and a heavy bass beat finds its way through cinderblocks and wallpaper. No matter where I sit in the apartment, I cannot find total silence. I decide to try the park. I aim for the tree furthest from any living thing, take a seat under it and close my eyes. The wind rustles the leaves, and through it I hear a distant siren. A squirrel, it can only be a squirrel, moves erratically around the trunk, and the clawing scuttle scratches at the string of silence onto which I try so hard to hold – until it snaps. Slightly annoyed, I leave the park and wander along noisy, bustling streets, keeping my eyes open for a haven of peace. Where in a city can one find silence? It's not in the sanctity of your own home, it's not in nature, it's not on the streets. I stop outside the synagogue. Without knowing how, my steps have taken me to Jewish God's house. Is a synagogue a church? Can I enter even though I'm not Jewish? I try to remember what my friend Ariel told me, about kosher and the little hats and the bread and the twirled hair. She took me to this place on the Lower East Side where they handed us, over a fat-stained counter that must have been a thousand years old , a heavy, doughy dumpling the size of a baseball. We ate the baseball, and I watched Ariel's nose hair flare as she chewed, and somehow it crept into my head that there were nose hairs in the ball, fallen from one of the lumpy-faced men behind the counter, and I couldn't bring myself to finish it.

Ariel asked me what was wrong, was I not enjoying it? "Tremendously," I said – for back then I hadn't learned the joy of rude honesty – and I swallowed the baseball, and the possible hair, in a couple of gulps. But for the love of things, I can't remember anything Ariel told me about being Jewish, so I make the sign of the cross and enter the synagogue. It's cool and empty inside, and I think I've finally found my place. I take a seat on a bench and close my eyes. At last I have it, silence. *Omertá*, the most respected quality of any Mafioso, the source and origin of everything, for what sounds could there have been when there was nothing? But then I hear it, a subtle drone from a distance, the sound one would have been thrilled to hear had one been cast away on a deserted island and desperate to hear the clippings of rotor blades, but not here in Jewish God's house. Whatever His name is, there's a fly in His house. It moves in and out but never comes close, and I try to block it out, ignore it and adopt a Zen-like approach, where the world is separate from my being and whatever happens there is a mere wave on the surface of a glass filled with water. But the stupid pill of a fly persists in such a convincing fashion: it seems to say, "Listen to me, world, forget all and listen to my buzzing," and in the surrounding silence it doubles, even triples in size, and I doubt very much that any Zen master in the world be disciplined enough to hear the silence underlying an attention-starved fly in a synagogue.

I leave and continue down the street in search of silence. It's now become a fixation: to find it, somewhere, just a slice of it, no matter how thin. But everywhere I turn there's only hustle and bustle, banging and rattling, rocking and rolling. I seem to be trapped in a sea of noise. Then, as I scan the headlines of a newspaper stand, I come to think of it. It's the mothership of all silences. Hush heaven with its twelve mute dwarfs, if you like. The library.

I pick up the pace and reach it in less than ten. Without looking I grab a book from a shelf and ask to be directed to the reading room.

And it's there, in the interval between the magnified scraping of turning pages, the rasping of paper fiber against flesh, that I discover it. Silence is constant, it is the wall to which everything that happens is fastened. Silence can't be found or heard because it is an inescapable part of each sound. Silence is everywhere, until a voice suddenly breaks it. "Are you having a baby?" An Asian girl is standing right beside my desk. "A baby?" I say, not getting it. "A baby," she says and nods at the book on my desk. It's *Your Baby, Week By Week,* and I get it. I ought to tell her about the search for silence, but instead I just shake my head and smile.

Her name is Jackie, and she's from China. She studies biology, or something in that general area, and we leave the library together. I get her number but never have to go through the whole hey, you want to get together sometime soon and do something? mating dance because she asks me if I like Goddard, and I say, "Goddard? I love Goddard," even though I really haven't seen any of his movies. If I had to guess I'd say they are artsy-fartsy and pretentious, but we decide to meet tomorrow at a movie theater in the West Village that is putting on this Goddard-fest as part of another French rama-lama-ding-dong.

But Goddard is yet eons away and I feel like a prima donna – not Liberace, but Elton John – as I prance home just to get ready for tonight's date. When did everything become all about meeting the perfect girl, the void-filler, the complete-maker? I suppose, when I think back, that it had already started in middle school. I'm not saying it has anything do to with hair growing on penises; I think it started long before that. It must have started when we began understanding, when we began seeing the light in our parents' eyes and understanding that it was a reflection of an emptiness deep inside. We noticed that emptiness in our parents, and even though we could sense it wasn't anything good, we were drawn to it with all our childish curiosity. It eluded us for some time, this locked vault in the secret land of grown-ups; then one day, as persistent children always do, we found our way through the maze and beheld it. It lay there, calm and inviting like a summer-night lake, and we could not help but to throw ourselves into it. And once you've dipped yourself in the lake, once you've gotten wet, the memory of it will always be there. So I have no choice but to get ready to meet Mallory.

I'm wearing a washed-out dark grey T-shirt with a Mickey Mouse print, and I've made sure to tell her so she can easily spot me. It works. She waves at me from the south side of Houston Street, just outside Whole Foods, and I cross the street trying to look cool, but in an unaffected way. We walk south, she in tall shoes with heels of checkered wood, and she begins telling me about her father. He is a judge in Philadelphia, and her mother is a housewife and her brother is a lawyer and she paints paintings and wants to make it on her own and is naturally considered the black sheep of the family. She talks as we move forward, I wouldn't say trying to find a place to eat, because we don't, we simply walk past restaurants on our way someplace that neither of us knows even exists. She has tattoos, but they break off in an interesting way against her pretty clothes. She wears a herringbone skirt and matching jacket, but the tattoos make it look more rock than Scarlett O'Hara. I say, just to say something, "What about here?" as we pass a place, and she, who is concerned that everything she does, as the black sheep she is, must come with a stamp of genuinity, as far away as possible from what her father would have wanted her to do, says, "I hate fancy places." Instead we get into a cab and go the four blocks over to the heart of the Lower East Side, because her feet hurt from walking on the checkered wood heels. Where we get out happens to be right in front of a small Thai place with an earthy interior and simple wood benches and tables. It fits the non-fancy standard, and we sit down halfway between the windows and the bathroom.

Mallory has the eyes of a cat, snakelike and deep, that automatically try to pull you in. I ask about the tattoo on her forearm, the one that looks like four jagged lines drawn next to each other to form a rectangle. She says she and her brother just got it one day: they drove Daddy's car to the poorer parts of town and got identical tattoos at a dive parlor as a silent protest against something undefined, perhaps making a stand against the Man. Not long afterward her brother had his lasered off, before the judge would catch the smell of ink. I show her my tattoo, and she digs it. Everybody does, so it's kind of a sure card to play, thus making it something I only rarely rely on. Not that I don't think things are going well – they are going as well as can be expected – I just don't know what I want. The only thing I'm sure of is what I want to eat – I order the spicy coconut shrimp – but with her, Mallory, and the other daisies, I haven't got a clue. But there's no alternative. I can't not not not not see anyone. I'm just saying, what if she one day sits there, across from me in a Thai restaurant with noodles hanging from a fork before her, and I find myself saying hallelujah, she's the one, the perfect one, a twenty-first century Cleopatra, what would I do? Would I marry her? Would I kill, mummify, and keep her forever in my closet? I don't know how you go about having someone, past the dinners and movies and handholding, how I would actually take the plunge that is

The Plunge? I think of this as I sit across from Mallory, who I'm fairly sure isn't the one, my Cleopatra, but who is nice enough to have noodles with, at least for one night. But what I want most of all is to figure out how I can get past this never-ending noodle-eating with strangers, the showing of my tattoo, the answering and asking of questions, always the million questions.

When we are done, we stand under a fire escape right across the street, even though it's not raining. Mallory pulls out a joint, and with the words, "I always do this out in the open," she lights it. With smoke still lingering from her parted lips she offers it up to me, and I take a modest puff, mostly not to be a wet rag. A sweet scent fills the air around us, and through it I lean and am received without resistance by her still-parted lips. Her tongue tastes salty from the food. A bubble begins to form around us, our own private universe. I don't know if it's the pot or the bubble of love, but the world around us ceases to exist. The bubble is still there – light and airy, translucent – when our faces part. "I do a lot of drugs," she says. In a flash her words set me straight. The background wall of reality slams down from above the scene, as the bubble, which was never a real bubble after all, disintegrates and disappears. It was the pot. When I walk her to the subway I try taking her hand, perhaps because I know she isn't the one and this is my way of comforting her (*There, there, you'll find someone soon.*) but she pulls it away with "I don't do handholding," and in my mind, only in my mind, I answer, *Yeah, but you do do drugs, don't you.* Above the entrance we kiss again, briefly, and this time time doesn't even acknowledge it, let alone pause for our benefit.

Sunday morning coming down, not for me but most likely for Mallory. Oh well, another day, another date. But it wasn't always like this. Sundays were once the king of the week, God's seventh magnificent wonder, and we spent them royally. We were the sovereign rulers of the Lord's day, she was our bitch and we rode her without mercy. Every drop possible we squeezed from her, and we lapped it up like greedy golden Labradors. Every now and then we'd stay in bed until after noon, and once we didn't get up at all, not until the morning after.

It was a glorious day. We sensed it would happen the night before and stayed up late, doing nothing special but preparing mentally. She woke first at around eight, rolled from my arms like a baby seal, hands and legs kept by her side, and then scooted with half-open eyes and sleepy feet towards the bathroom. I knew I should get up and go right after her, or I would suffer serious sleep-in bladder, but when she came scooting back, still seal-bodied, and rolled herself right back into my arms, I decided I'd gladly let my bladder suffer. I lasted until about nine thirty, and when I came back I crawled in from the foot of the bed, under the duvet, sniffing my way through clouds of down until I found her. I pulled her panties down and offered them with one hand to the floor before I laid my body on top of hers and interrupted her slumber by sucking on her lower lip. We made love, first very slowly, so as not to disturb sleep, and completely submerged under the duvet. But, little by little, I chased her up towards the headboard, joined together hipwise until we lay completely open and free under what Sunday light managed to creep in through the shades. Afterward we rested on our backs, panting our way down to zero again. Trickles of light shot through the air and illuminated penny-sized areas of her body, where tiny drops of sweat lay in orderly mounds, vibrating slightly as they evaporated. We ordered breakfast from the café around the corner, and only when the doorbell rang did I put on underwear. She hid under the covers. We ate cream cheese bagels and cheese tortillas and drank chai and freshly squeezed orange juice, resting against the same headboard that had only moments ago supported our sweaty bodies. For us it seemed like eons ago. After breakfast we brushed the bed free of crumbs and slumbered again to the soothing sounds of Gustavo Santaolalla finger-picking his guitar. We awoke, we visited the bathroom, we made love, we ordered lunch, we watched reruns of *Seinfeld*, *Friends,* and *Roseanne*, and we did it all over again for dinner. Not once did we touch the shades to look outside, open a window, or turn on our phones. The bed was our life raft, complete with takeout and remote controls, but still a life raft, and we clung to it like two capsized sailors never wanting to spot land again.

I arrive at the movie theater early and wait in the lobby. I gaze at posters from the past, some of which are from movies I've seen, others not. As I admire the poster for Hitchcock's *The 39 Steps,* the 1959 color remake with a man peeling away a curtain to reveal a steaming locomotive, I feel a tap on my shoulder. It's library Jackie. She is wearing a black beret, the exact same color of her hair, and it traces the outline of her face perfectly. *She has a nasty habit of sneaking up on you,* I think and see that the rest of her outfit is also black, every single piece but for her shoes, which are red. She looks very avant-garde. The Goddard movie starts as soon as we sit down, even though people are still working their way towards their seats. It seems the French have a low tolerance for tardiness. I've always envisioned them to be quite the opposite, a *comme ci, comme ça* set of people, intent on sucking down the oysters of life with a Gauloises carelessly hung from the corner of the mouth. *Perhaps the projectionist is German,* I think and let the movie sweep me away. I should say, I *try* to let it sweep me, but not much sweeping occurs. There's no plot, only a bunch of scenes threaded together in succession. There's a man – a loudmouthed, wide-shouldered, square-jawed American – a woman, friends of the woman, Italy, a red sports car, convertible, that will in the end be the loudmouthed American's downfall as he is beheaded crashing into a truck.

The only part of the movie that manages to move me is the house. It is a magnificent house perched on top of a cliff right by the sparkling Mediterranean. The futuristic-looking dwelling is the kind Ernst Stavro Blofeld would have inhabited without shame, with large round windows that never cease staring out at the surrounding vastness, and on top of it all, naturally, is the roof. The roof doubles as a terrace, and its grey cement finish covers everything: the wind shelter, the lounge chairs, and a partition behind which there's an outdoor shower. It could well be the roof of a space station, although a space station set in marvelous surroundings, for below it all shines the jewel-encrusted surface of the sea. This house is the only thing in the movie that talks to me, and it seems to say, *Forget everything about everything, my rooftop terrace is all you'll ever need.* It is so convincing that at that precise moment I wouldn't have minded trading everything for a lifetime on that rooftop.

The lights come on the moment the last frame ends. It's decidedly a German projectionist, and one who is in a rush to get out of there – perhaps he has a date waiting in the lobby or already sitting by a lonesome table in a restaurant. Jackie and I squeeze through the crowd outside and manage to get the first cab. And despite the fact that a) I'm not in the mood for even beginning the laborious job of unfolding her excess of black avant-garde cloth just to get laid, and b) I live in the opposite direction, I say, I'm going in the same direction, let's share a cab. And despite it all we kiss in the back of the car, the taxi driver ogling us with his one lazy eye (a syndrome brought on by excessive ogling?), and when we stand outside her building, the taxi has sped off and I bid Jackie goodnight with yet another kiss, I feel utterly stupid. Stupid and weak for being again and again caught up in the net of desire. When she's gone I stand there for quite some time, waiting for a cab to pass, before I accept defeat and start walking towards the nearest subway station.

TWELFTH CHAPTER

During the weekend, hackers entered the computer system at work and wreaked havoc, so the office is spilling over with programming engineers when I get in on Monday. It seems they've been here 24/7, for empty cartons of pizza, Coke bottles, and coffee cups litter the entire place. I get to my desk unnoticed and mentally seal myself off. I focus and have the entire floor to myself. In fact, the entire city of New York has been hit by a deadly virus, leaving only cynical, brokenhearted men between the ages of thirty and thirty-three alive. It's me and a couple of queers from the Village left, but in this very building I'm all alone. I could work away to my heart's content, naked if I wished, but I settle for diving into the next barrel of links.

SMALL TALK

Small talk is an informal type of discourse that does not cover any functional topics of conversation or any transactions that need to be addressed. Small talk is conversation for its own sake, or

"... comments on what is perfectly obvious." The phenomenon of small talk was initially studied in 1923 by Bronisław Malinowski, who coined the term "phatic communication" to describe it. The ability to conduct small talk is a social skill, hence small talk is some type of social communication.

In spite of seeming to have little useful purpose, small talk is a bonding ritual and a strategy for managing interpersonal distance. It serves many functions in helping to define the relationships between friends, work colleagues, and new acquaintances. In particular, it helps new acquaintances to explore and categorize each other's social position. Small talk is closely related to the need for people to maintain positive face – to feel approved-of by those who are listening to them.

In some conversations there is no specific functional or informative element at all. The following example of small talk is between two colleagues who pass each other in a hallway:

William : Morning, Paul.
Paul : Oh, morning, William, how are you?
William : Fine, thanks. Have a good weekend?
Paul : Yes, thanks. Catch you later.
William : OK, see you.

This type of discourse is often called chatter.

Speech patterns between women tend to be more collaborative than those of men, and tend to support each other's involvement in the conversation. Topics for small talk are more likely to include compliments about some aspect of personal appearance. For example, "That dress really suits you." Small talk between women who are friends may also involve a greater degree of self disclosure. Topics may cover more personal aspects of their life, their troubles, and their secrets. This self-disclosure both generates a closer relationship between them, and also is a signal of that closeness.

By contrast, men's small talk tends to be more competitive. It may feature **verbal sparring matches**, playful insults, and putdowns.

VERBAL SPARRING MATCHES – REDIRECTED: **STICHOMYTHIA**

Stichomythia is a technique in verse drama in which single alternating lines, or half-lines, are given to alternating characters.

Stichomythia is particularly well suited to sections of dramatic dialogue where two characters are in violent dispute. The rhythmic intensity of the alternating lines combined with quick, biting ripostes in the dialogue can be quite powerful.

An example from film is in *Double Indemnity* where Walter Neff flirts with Phyllis Dietrichson; she resists him.

Dietrichson: You were anxious to talk to [my husband] weren't you?

Neff: Yeah, I was, but I'm sort of getting over the idea, if you know what I mean.

Dietrichson: There's a speed limit in this state, Mr. Neff, 45 miles an hour.

Neff: How fast was I going officer?

Dietrichson: I'd say around 90.

Neff: Suppose you get down off your motorcycle and give me a ticket?

Dietrichson: Suppose I let you off with a warning this time?

Neff: Suppose it doesn't take?

Dietrichson: Suppose I have to whack you over the knuckles?

Neff: Suppose I bust out crying and put my head on your shoulder?

Dietrichson: Suppose you try putting it on my husband's shoulder?

Neff: That tears it!

In the prose context of most film, stichomythia has been defined as a "witty exchange of one-liners" and associated with the film noir characters Jeff Bailey in Out of the Past, Sam Spade, and **Philip Marlowe.**

PHILIP MARLOWE

Philip Marlowe is a fictional character created by Raymond Chandler in a series of novels including *The Big Sleep* and *The Long Goodbye*. Marlowe first appeared under that name in *The Big Sleep* published in 1939.

Underneath the wisecracking, hard drinking, tough private eye, Marlowe is quietly contemplative and philosophical and enjoys chess and poetry. While he is not afraid to risk physical harm, he does not dish out violence merely to settle scores. Morally upright, he is not fooled by the genre's usual femmes fatale, such as Carmen Sternwood in *The Big Sleep*.

Chandler was said to have taken the name Marlowe from Marlowe House, to which he belonged during his time at **Dulwich College**.

DULWICH COLLEGE

Dulwich College is an independent school for boys in Dulwich, southeast London, England. The college was founded in 1619 by Edward Alleyn, a successful Elizabethan actor, with the original purpose of educating 12 poor scholars as the foundation of "God's Gift".

The school has a very extensive archive, especially of material relating to drama and the arts. Other interesting artifacts held by the college include the "James Caird", the whaler in which Ernest Shackleton made his intrepid voyage for survival to South Georgia from **Elephant Island** in 1916.

ELEPHANT ISLAND

Elephant Island is an ice-covered, mountainous island off the coast of Antarctica in the outer reaches of the South Shetland Islands in the Southern Ocean. Its name was given by early explorers sighting **elephant seals** on its shores.

ELEPHANT SEALS

Elephant seals (sea elephants) are large, oceangoing seals in the genus *Mirounga*. Elephant seals take their name from the large proboscis of the adult males (bulls) which resembles an elephant's trunk. The bull's proboscis is used in producing extraordinarily loud roaring noises, especially during the mating season.

Elephant seals spend upwards of 80% of their lives in the ocean. They can hold their breath for more than 100 minutes

– longer than any other noncetacean mammal. Elephant seals dive to 1550 m beneath the ocean's surface. Elephant seals are shielded from extreme cold by their **blubber**, more so than by fur.

BLUBBER

Blubber is a thick layer of vascularized adipose tissue found under the skin of all cetaceans, pinnipeds and sirenians. It can comprise up to 50% of the body mass of some marine mammals during some points in their lives, and can range from two inches (5 cm) thick in dolphins and smaller whales, to more than 12 inches (30 cm) thick in some bigger whales.

Blubber differs from other forms of adipose tissue in its extra thickness, which allows it to serve as an efficient thermal insulator, making blubber essential for thermoregulation. See also **Globster.**

GLOBSTER

A globster, or blob, is an unidentified organic mass that washes up on the shoreline of an ocean or other body of water. The term was coined by Ivan T. Sanderson in 1962 to describe the Tasmanian carcass of 1960, which was said to have "no visible eyes, no defined head, and no apparent bone structure".

A globster is distinguished from a normal beached carcass by being hard to identify, at least by initial untrained observers, and by creating controversy as to its identity.

In the past these were often described as sea monsters, and myths and legends about such monsters may often have started with the appearance of a globster. Globsters are most frequently studied in the field of **cryptozoology**.

CRYPTOZOOLOGY

Cryptozoology (from Greek *kryptos*, "hidden" + zoology; literally, "study of hidden animals") refers to the search for animals whose existence has not been proven. This includes looking for living examples of animals that are considered extinct, such as dinosaurs; animals whose existence lacks physical evidence but which appear in myths, legends, or are reported, such as Bigfoot and Chupacabra; and wild animals dramatically outside their normal geographic ranges, such as **phantom cats** or "ABCs" (an initialism commonly used by cryptozoologists that stands for Alien Big Cats).

PHANTOM CATS

Phantom cats, also known as Alien Big Cats (ABCs), are large felines, such as jaguars or cougars, which have been purported to appear in regions outside their indigenous range. Sightings, tracks and predation have been reported in a number of countries and states including Britain, Australia, Ireland, New Zealand, Finland, Denmark, Hawaii, and **Luxembourg**.

We like things we recognize. I, for instance, never like records the first time I listen to them. It's always after the second or third time that they get me, if they get me at all. I need to be wined and dined by melody and text for the right synapses to develop in my brain. Perhaps that's the essence of my problem right there, that I never even make it to the second listening. All these first spins, the popping of the audio cherry, with each note, each bridge, word, and chorus as unfamiliar as a newly laid train track. A train track that reaches far into the wilderness. And it's an uncomfortable ride, too, because there are so many things to think about as the very first passenger. For instance, whether one has chosen the proper attire. And if the scenery is drab, the question of whether the trip will be very long of course arises. Heading into the unknown is a strenuous task, and then I haven't even approached the subject of meeting the natives.

On the other hand, perhaps that is exactly what I am looking for, a first-listening kind of girl, one with whom the tune instantly makes sense and the chorus sticks already after the first verse. Problem is that these records only come along very rarely, when the stars align and music gods are high on amphetamines. Factoring out dating ad after lifeless dating ad, I have but one fear, and that is getting stuck in a perpetual state of dating. Like the movie *Groundhog Day,* except Punxsutawney Phil is no longer a groundhog but a New York gal with a bachelor's degree in marketing, or publishing, or fashion design, or law, or blah blah and yuckety blah. And it's true, they are all the same. Even though their appearances may differ slightly, and that's slightly with a slippery *s* because they are all pre-packed in the same factory. We are all the children of marketers. Today there no longer exist any unsoiled virgins.

I'd hate that, I'd really hate that, to get stuck in the very thing I loathe the most. I see it all the time: statistics show that more than 70 percent of those who are with us today have been with us for at least two years. The conclusion is frightening. It's not just about finding someone, it's about being part of the huffing and puffing chance machine, about never stopping to look for the perfect one. Is there even such a thing? one might ask. Well, my company packages, sells, and delivers just that. I'm beginning to believe that's the real problem, the dream weavers like myself who make you believe in storybook endings. "Marketers are fucking evil," the ever-so-bitter comedian Bill Hicks said. And isn't that true? If you think about it, if there is one trait we value most of all traits in our modern world, it's the ability to sell things to other people. If you can do that, in whatever field, you are king.

But it's not because of evil marketers or Bill Hicks that I've decided to try something radical, but because I'm scared to death of ending up like Bill Murray, reliving one never-ending, never-evolving date for the rest of my life. I have decided that I will only go on three more dates, and if I don't find my first-listening wonder I will call it quits. No more dates, ever. And while I'm at it I make another vow. If I haven't found someone in three dates I will quit my job.

Diane asks me if I've heard about the hacking and I tell her the truth.

It was me.

Her answer makes me laugh out loud.

Good
riddance.

I want to tell Diane about my new three-date policy, but then I recall our last attempt at chumminess and don't. Instead I tell her about the blubber, and the phantom cats, and also about small talk. We practice it a wee bit, in honor of hairdressers, aunties, and salesmen all over the country.

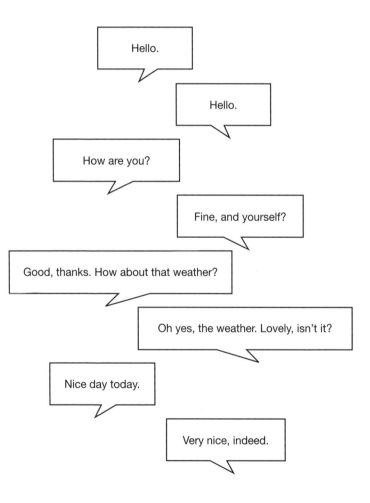

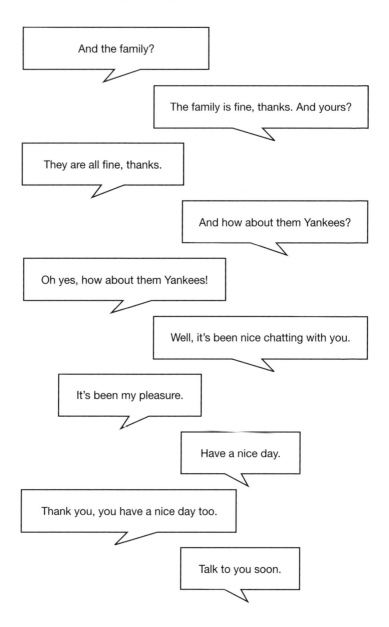

And the family?

The family is fine, thanks. And yours?

They are all fine, thanks.

And how about them Yankees?

Oh yes, how about them Yankees!

Well, it's been nice chatting with you.

It's been my pleasure.

Have a nice day.

Thank you, you have a nice day too.

Talk to you soon.

When Diane and I are done with today's pleasantries, the phatic conversation ends and I dump out a fuckload of ads for the company. I get into such a groove that I work nonstop until way past lunch. When I finally sit with my sandwich in the square in front of the entrance I am so jacked up with the words of fake personas that my mind can't help spinning them out for whoever I see. A black man crosses the square, calmly and with great confidence. He holds his head high, and the suit makes no attempt to crumple on his straight back. I begin chiseling out a profile about an entertainment lawyer, a former college football star who likes soul – the music, not the food or the spiritual stuff – tae kwon do, and Hugo Boss, and can make a mean California roll. From the opposite side of the square, leaving the building and almost brushing against my Nubian brother, comes a woman, perhaps forty-five years old, with a stocky build and curly black hair, wearing dark sunglasses, walking with a slight limp. My mind sprints and jumps over hurdles for the unsuspecting woman. She works in insurance, a broker of some sort, and in her spare time she's very fond of water sports (not the urinary kind, but the H_2O ones – they make her feel light and thin, but she doesn't put that in her ad) and she'll do anything from canoeing to snorkeling, with the exception of waterskiing, which an old hip injury prevents her from enjoying. She likes music, fine dining, and wine, and she holds a membership to the Guggenheim. She wants to meet someone genuine and caring, with no children. She has a cat named Lizzy. Wherever I look ads automatically bubble up to the surface, and to keep from going bananas I finish my sandwich while staring at a gum stain on the ground right next to my foot.

Back at my desk I am determined to choose my next date wisely. Thirty-three percent, that's the amount of fuel I will burn on each mission, and if I don't manage to reach the mothership in three attempts, that's it. No more Captain Kirk for me. The Death Star will gobble me up. As I look through my options I am interrupted by a pimple-faced young man who sticks his head over the side of my prism. He wants to know if I've experienced anything strange with the system. I know I shouldn't, but I can't help spinning it. "I think the current economic system eventually will violate our relationships to resources, such as the convention of property. There will always be problems of allocation and scarcity of resources." Pimple Face blinks at me, and for a moment I think his head will simply fall off the wall, hit the floor on my side with a thud, and roll for a few revolutions until it comes to a halt against my foot. I realize I have encountered stupidity and try to smooth things over with some phatic conversation. "Hey, how about that discontinuation of Jolt Cola?" But Pimple Face's face is blank, apart from the pimples that stare at me with angry red eyes. "System is fine," I finally say, and his head does fall off but luckily rolls over the other side of the wall.

A couple of hours later I know what I had suspected after only ten minutes – I made the wrong choice. Somewhere after the Andromeda Galaxy I took the wrong exit, and swoosh there I go, heading directly for a black hole. It has nothing to do with her personality, or perhaps it has everything to do with it. Simply put, Lisa is a bitch in heat. The night is a jumble of cabs, houses, and rooms, but everything starts with an ordinary dinner. Lisa eats corn on the cob, and she does it like it is a cock. It's not just my imagination: the father at the table next to us stares at her sensual table manners whenever he is sure his wife, who by the way tucks away load after load of food in her cheeks like some monstrous hamster, isn't looking. The corn-blowing aside, I try to concentrate on what Lisa is telling me between slobbers. She talks about Korea. She describes the subway there as something Apple might have built: shiny, white, and sleek, where recordings of birds chirping announce each stop. The biggest sport in Korea (you'd think it was cock-sucking) is playing video games, and big games are broadcast in giant stadiums on giant screens with a hundred thousand spectators in the stands, cheering and bleeping. What's even more insane is that every now and then, in one of the endless gaming places housed in dark basements with vending machines selling all kinds of weird fish-flavored snacks, some kid keels over and dies in the middle of pushing sticky control buttons. They die from malnutrition, having pressed their bodies too far on nothing but caffeine and, at best, the salty fish snacks. By the time we have finished eating and the check arrives I feel pretty up to date on Korea, and I know how to say at least five words, one of them being *hello*, and like an exalted penny falling through a slot, finally I make sense of the little Korean boy, Annyong, in *Arrested Development*.

With a snappy jingle, a sitcom scene-change, we are on our way in a cab to Lisa's friend's birthday party. Her hand finds mine in the backseat, and it's not long, after a short meet-and-greet and a polite sampling of a vile, lime-green birthday cake, that our tongues also meet in the strange darkness behind a closed door. Her face is soft and plump to the touch, like an Eskimo's, and while our mouths discuss the latest news our hands wander blindly, an automated response in my case, in a race to remove the necessary clothing. Meanwhile, there's an elusive detail that stands out. When we fall into a stranger's bed, her blouse opened just enough and her bra pushed down but not removed, skirtless and pantyless, and I, almost like the joke about the cheating husband and the screaming wife, literally fall forward and prick her bull's-eye with my prick, I realize what it is. She is scentless. Not a whiff of smell escapes her. She could have been made of sterilized water, had I not known better, and even in the midst of passion I can't help but brood over this curious fact. Perhaps it is something Korean, somehow linked to the futuristic subway system? I don't have time to ponder long, for a sharp knock on the door has us up and grabbing for our clothes, and it's a small wonder when we exit the room in two shakes of a lamb's tail, myself slightly flushed, that each of us is wearing what we wore going in.

The smaller party then moves to a larger party, and I again find myself in a cab. We are three in the back and one in the front, plus the driver, who wears the same cologne my grandfather doused himself in. It feels like we are part of yet another joke, this time the one about how many people you can fit in a cab. Legs are touching legs, elbows squeezed against elbows, and if we all inhale simultaneously, we expand against the car doors until we sit wedged in a vise-tight grip. Consequently there's no room for kissing, something Lisa makes up for as soon as we get out. While our companions join the trickle of people leading into the house, Lisa holds me back and plants one right on my lips. It's as if she's, for eternities, been starved of all human contact, and now that the gates are open every drop of pent-up lust comes gushing out. Her mouth is raping mine, her tongue and lips devouring everything in their path. When she starts fumbling with my fly I manage to remove myself from her sucking power and suggest we go inside.

It's a regular house party with people everywhere, music and booze. Lisa heads directly upstairs and I follow, not like a puppy on a string, but like a moth to a flame. She's a sexual SWAT team, her eyes scanning each space as we move forward, and when we come upon the empty bathroom she pushes me inside with one swift and commanding movement.

This time we leave our clothes on. She simply lifts her skirt up, her panties are mysteriously lost, and I drop my pants to my ankles. We begin anew, with me sitting on the closed toilet lid and her on top of me. As the toilet isn't properly fixed to the floor, it waddles from side to side, causing the water tank to hiss and spit behind my back. Lisa seem oblivious to the fact and moves her hips back and forth so hard I'm worried the toilet will give any second and we will both be tumbling in a geyser of water. Call it faith or karma, but once again there's a knock on the door and a loud booming voice demands to be let in. *Here we go,* I think as Lisa gets off me in a jiffy, and not even a second after I've pulled my pants up she opens the door without so much as a crease of emotion in her face.

We continue on our journey – for it is a journey, a quest even, for a place to fuck in peace. Not so much for me – I'm actually at peace, and the sex is only clouding my mind and draining focus from my real mission – but for Lisa, who seems determined to finish what she started. Back downstairs we pass through throngs of bodies, through a living room that stinks of cat piss, into the kitchen, where we exit through the back door. I walk behind and have plenty of time to take notice of Lisa's head. I haven't thought of it before, but it's curiously huge, sumo-shaped, and the more I stare at it the bigger it gets. *Perhaps it's the interrupted sex, passion rerouted, that has caused it to swell,* I think.

In the backyard we find only traces of others in the form of three plastic cups filled with beer and soggy cigarette butts, and Lisa, a wolf in heat, leans her big head back and sniffs the air. She seems to be content with what she learns; if she had a tail I'm sure it would have wagged.

She drags me to the narrow maintenance path that runs alongside the house, and there, like a cowboy or a railway worker, she brusquely puts her one foot up on the bottom edge of the central air pump, lifts her skirt to reveal a black, silky kitty, and whispers almost electrically, "Fuck me." What can I do but her? And I do. With one eye on her now-enormous head, I keep the other trained on the backyard in case someone decides to come knocking on this door, too, and enter her standing. We bump and grind, and she moans and sticks her tongue deep into my ear. But something is off. Perhaps it's the scentlessness, the lack of pheromones and whatnot, and I concentrate hard to finish, for I can't bear another scavenging hunt for a new place. *You've come a long way, don't blow it now,* I tell myself, and that's what I do. I blow myself right on her inner thigh, and the moment I do I realize something is wrong. My manhood, my once clean and proud member, is covered in blood. It looks more like a newborn baby than the apple of my eye. "Oh shit," is all she says, "it came." Slightly disgusted, yet satisfied to be done with it, I only stand in silence as she uses my tank top to wipe herself clean. When I've done the same I toss the bloodied package over the fence and hope no one finds it and uses my sperm for any unethical military research programs. If they do, they should know that my aim is as bad on the shooting range as with women, so someone better have a tank to hide behind.

Not long after, at least not long enough, when SWAT Lisa again begins trotting around the house on the lookout for an empty room, a closet, or even a plastic bag, I tell her I'm all out of tank tops and hit the road. The harsh subway light turns the ride home into an extraterrestial experience. Somehow it's different at night, even though down there it's always dark, and when I get home I fall asleep as soon as I hit the bed.

Like Jamiroquai once said, everything is virtual reality. When I wake up from my dream I'm not sure what is dream and what is reality. Is reality walking with my ex through the corn maze in New Jersey, and did I only dream about the date with Lisa, the bleeding nymphomaniac? I lift the covers and look down at my naked body, and there I see the indisputable marks of reality – flakes of crusted blood falling off my penis. That means I'm not sure there ever was a corn maze. Perhaps there never was an ex-girlfriend? I get up and begin looking for clues to her existence. I find nothing in the bedroom, only scattered images in my head as I picture her face and body on things. Is it possible everything's just been a mental projection? That I have made it all up? Even though I distinctly remember throwing everything out, I go to the kitchen and look for the potato-masher jimmy, I search the fridge door for affirmations and I even look in the bathroom for the pirate-skull bucket, but everything is gone. I have rid myself of her. Suddenly I feel like I've lost my footing. What if, horrid thought, that's all there is? Mere thoughts? What if raccoon-hatted Jay Kay was right? There's really only one way to find out. Without further ado I decide I have go back to the cornfield. I need to anchor my memories in reality, in something tangible. I need to reboot my system so I know if I'm awake or if I'm dreaming.

I work through lunch. I have decided to take the four o'clock train that leaves from Penn Station. But at three I get so nervous about the whole thing that I text Frank, and I have to say, I've never been so happy to see half a person waiting for me on the platform, and together we enter the tunnel leading to the magical land of gardens.

You'd think the air would be different in New Jersey. Well, perhaps you don't, but I always do, clearing a state line and all, but it's really the same as in New York. I close the window and watch it looming in the distance like some Superman metropolis that we've managed to escape before it blows, and I let the train's rhythmic beating calm me down. Frank falls asleep, and for a moment I think that he will glide out of his seat and end up in a lump on the floor, but he never actually gets past the bottom hump and sits perched there, smoothed out against the seat bottom. I have plenty of time to think about the corn maze.

We took the train – in fact, it could have been this very train – and I remember that even though I wasn't wearing a straw hat and a plaid shirt, my insides felt empty as a scarecrow's. There was a distance, an invisible barrier between us that had crept up without warning. One day it was just there. It was nothing words could describe, we both still smiled and we still kissed, but there was a crack through which our light seeped, and however I searched I couldn't find it. An outing, a joyous late-summer carnival in the fertile farmlands, that was a way to momentarily escape the city and our life together there.

Frank does fall to the floor as the train pulls into our stop, but it's not the train's movement but my hand on his shoulder that startles him. From the station we take a bus, and after another twenty-five minutes we arrive at the farm. It's changed since I was last here, I notice right away. Now a big sign at the entrance announces the Walk of Death, where actor zombies lurch and reach for you through the disguise and confusion of yellow cornstalks. Thank god it's not on for another couple of weeks. The maze is open, though, and I pay for myself and Frank to walk it. "Listen," I tell him, for he hasn't even asked me why we are here. "There's something I have to do, so you go on ahead and I'll take my time." It's a gray and gloomy day; tenebrous clouds have gathered in the distance, but the forecast doesn't call for any rain. Then again, what does anybody know about rain? If it rains, it rains.

I watch Frank leave, his body not even half the height of the gangly cornstalks, and soon they have swallowed him up completely. A family of four stands over by the produce wagon, selecting corn by pointing at one at a time, as if none of them can speak. Other than that it's deserted. It's just me and the corn maze.

When we were here it was a busy day, with kids running screaming all around the farm. But once we had walked halfway into the maze and stood captured in the middle of the giant field, it was nearly dead quiet. There was only a slight whisper from the corn. I step into the maze and start walking. Beyond the first bend my impressions are already reduced to only three things: the trampled dirt path strewn with withered hay below me, the surrounding cornstalks, and the sky above. All else is left in the outside world. It's what I'd imagine it would be walking through a video game where all you hear are your own footsteps, and all you see is the next turn and the next after that. I don't see another living soul, not even a bird in the sky, but still I find the spot without problem. It's about halfway in, right after a sharp bend that has you walking back in the direction you just came from, where a wooden stake, most likely the remnants of an old fencepost, sits hidden behind a particularly dense patch of corn. I'm not yet sure if this is really my third time here, but I have no problem finding it. I don't even have to count my steps from the turn to know exactly where to start digging. An ant scurries away from my fingers as they burrow through the dirt, and about five inches deep I unearth it. It's somewhat weathered – I never thought of covering it in a plastic bag – and a thin layer of oxidation has begun to overtake it. It wasn't supposed to sit here so long. I hold the ring between my thumb and my forefinger, and right then, among the cornstalks towering all around me, the once-distant clouds that have come together above my head release their loads, and I let the rain rinse the dirt off my hands.

By the time I make it back to the farm I am completely soaked. It's stopped raining, and I'm not sure if I should laugh or cry. Not about the rain, but about my life. In a way I should be happy that it all wasn't just a dream, that it actually did happen. I should be happy that I am not crazy for imagining. But not being crazy also means that I did once have something precious that I no longer have, and that all that remains of her is an unused and slightly soiled engagement ring. But right now I'm cold and empty, and I decide to postpone my decision until later. I try to locate Frank but he's nowhere to be seen. I look all over the farm for him; I ask the young boy who sold us tickets, I ask the clerks in the gift store and in the bakery, but nobody has seen him. By the time I have walked the entire maze again my clothes are dry and the daylight is fading. I'm not sure what to do. He doesn't answer his phone, and when the last bus pulls in I have no choice but to get on it. I text Frank that I'll see him in the city.

As it turns out I don't have to choose. The ride home is tainted by sadness as I relive the moment when we walked the corn maze. I was so excited that my heart raced, but I kept a straight face, and when we came to the sharp turn there was…nothing. Teresa got a text message and became engaged in replying with great fervor, as if the text had come as a saving grace, to take her out of the godforsaken field, out of my life, and put her down in the city with her kind. Where she belonged. And I just couldn't do it. We walked past the spot where I had been only two days earlier, the turned soil still damp, and I didn't have the guts to stop her, to say, listen, put your phone down and listen to me, I want this to work. But I didn't say anything, and the moment we passed the sharp turn in the middle of the maze it was as if we entered another world completely. A world where we were no longer lovers.

Frank hasn't called me back, and I check my phone every hour to be sure not to miss him. I keep the ring in my office drawer, next to a box of paperclips and an obsolete bottle of Tipp-Ex, the typist's once-upon-a-time magical helper. I'm not sure what could have happened to him. Most likely he walked the maze, tired of waiting for me, and went back to the city. Maybe his phone ran out of power and he hasn't had time to charge it. I'm not really worried. I tell myself this as I fight off images of an enormous eagle swooping down from the heavens, picking Frank up in its sharp claws and carrying him away, screaming. But I decide not to worry. Stress is a killer, *they* say, and when *they* talk, you'd better listen. To keep any bad thoughts at bay I concentrate on producing an efficient number of ads and spend the rest of the day linking.

LUXEMBOURG

Luxembourg, officially the Grand Duchy of Luxembourg, is a landlocked country in western Europe, bordered by Belgium, France, and Germany.

Luxembourg is one of the smallest countries in Europe, and ranked 175th in size of all the 194 independent countries of the world; the country is about 2,586 square kilometers (998 sq mi) in size, and measures 82 km (51 miles) long and 57 km (35 miles) wide. It lies between latitudes 49° and **51° N**, and longitudes 5° and 7° E.

51° N

The 51st parallel north is a circle of latitude that is 51 degrees north of the Earth's equatorial plane. It crosses Europe, Asia, the Pacific Ocean, North America, and the Atlantic Ocean.

At this latitude the sun is visible for 16 hours, 33 minutes during the **summer solstice** and 7 hours, 55 minutes during the winter solstice.

SUMMER SOLSTICE

The summer solstice occurs exactly when the Earth's semi-axis in a given hemisphere is most inclined towards the sun, at its maximum tilt of 23° 26'. Though the summer solstice is an instant in time, the term is also colloquially used like Midsummer to refer to the day on which it occurs. Except in the polar regions (where daylight is continuous for many months), the day on which the summer solstice occurs is the day of the year with the longest period of daylight. The summer solstice occurs in June in the Northern Hemisphere north of the **Tropic of Cancer** (23° 26'N) and in December in the Southern Hemisphere south of the Tropic of Capricorn (23° 26'S).

TROPIC OF CANCER

Tropic of Cancer is a novel by Henry Miller, first published in 1934 by the Obelisk Press in Paris, France. Its publication in 1961 in the United States by Grove Press led to an obscenity trial – one of several that tested American laws on pornography in the 1960s.

The book was distributed by Frances Steloff at her **Gotham Book Mart**, in defiance of censorship pressures.

GOTHAM BOOK MART

The Gotham Book Mart, in operation from 1920 to 2007, was a famous midtown Manhattan bookstore and cultural landmark. Known for its distinctive sign above the door which read, "Wise Men Fish Here" (sign created by artist John Held, Jr.), the business was located first in a small basement space on West 45th Street near the Theater District, it then moved to 51 West 47th Street, then spent many years at 41 West 47th Street within the **Diamond District** in Manhattan, New York City, before finally moving to 16 East 46th Street.

THE DIAMOND DISTRICT

The Diamond District is an area of New York City located on West 47th Street between Fifth Avenue and Sixth Avenue (Avenue of the Americas) in midtown Manhattan.

It has been reported that total receipts for the value of a single day's trade on the block average $400 million. There are 2,600 independent businesses located in the district, nearly all of them dealing in diamonds or jewelry. Most are located in booths at one of the 25 "exchanges" in the district. Many deals are finalized by a simple, traditional blessing (*mazel und brucha*) and handshake. The Diamond Dealers Club – also known as the DDC – is an exclusive club that acts as a de facto **diamond** exchange and has its own synagogue.

DIAMOND

A diamond (from the ancient Greek – *adámas*, meaning "unbreakable," "proper," or "unalterable") is one of the best-known and most sought-after gemstones. Diamonds have been known to humankind and used as decorative items since ancient times; some of the earliest references can be traced to India.

The hardness of diamond and its high dispersion of light – giving the diamond its characteristic "fire" – make it useful for industrial applications and desirable as jewelry. Diamonds are such a highly traded commodity that multiple organizations have been created for grading and certifying them based on the four Cs, which are carat, cut, color, and clarity.

Historically, it has been claimed that diamonds possess several supernatural powers:

A diamond gives victory to he or she who carries it bound on his left arm, no matter the number of enemies.

Panics, pestilences, enchantments, all fly before it; hence, it is good for sleepwalkers and the **insane.**

INSANITY

Insanity, craziness or madness is a spectrum of behaviors characterized by certain abnormal mental or behavioral patterns. Insanity may manifest as violations of societal norms, including becoming a danger to themselves and others, though not all such acts are considered insanity.

Europe's oldest asylum is the Bethlem Royal Hospital of London, also known as Bedlam, which began admitting the mentally ill in 1403. The first American asylum was built in Williamsburg, Virginia, circa 1773. Before the 19th century these hospitals were used to isolate the mentally ill or the socially ostracized from society rather than cure them or maintain their health. Pictures from this era portrayed patients bound with rope or chains, often to beds or walls, or restrained in **straitjackets**.

STRAITJACKET

A straitjacket is a garment shaped like a jacket with overlong sleeves and is typically used to restrain a person who may otherwise cause harm to themselves or others. Once the arms are inserted into the straitjacket's sleeves, they are then crossed across the chest. The ends of the sleeves are then tied to the back of the wearer, ensuring that the arms are kept close to the chest with as little movement as possible.

Although *straitjacket* is the most common spelling, *strait-jacket* is also frequently used, and in Scotland *strait-waistcoat*, which is generally deemed archaic. Straitjackets are also known as camisoles.

The straitjacket's effectiveness as a restraint makes it of special interest in escapology. The straitjacket is also a staple prop in stage magic and is sometimes used in **bondage** games.

BONDAGE

Bondage is the use of restraints for the sexual pleasure of the parties involved. It may be used in its own right, as in the case of rope bondage and breast bondage, or as part of sexual activity or BDSM activity.

A subculture of gay men, sometimes called **leathermen**, were arguably among the first group to make obvious hints of their tastes in bondage in public.

LEATHERMEN – REDIRECTED: LEATHER SUBCULTURE

The leather subculture denotes practices and styles of dress organized around sexual activities. Wearing leather garments is one way that participants in this culture self-consciously distinguish themselves from mainstream sexual cultures. Leather culture is most visible in gay communities and most often associated with gay men ("leathermen"), but it is also reflected in various ways in the gay, lesbian, bisexual, and straight worlds.

But for others, wearing black leather clothing is an erotic fashion that expresses heightened masculinity or the appropriation of sexual power; love of motorcycles and independence; and/or engagement in sexual kink or leather fetishism.

Perhaps no figure has more vividly represented the leather subculture in the popular imagination than the leatherman portrayed by Glenn Hughes of the **Village People**.

VILLAGE PEOPLE

Village People is a concept disco group formed in the United States in 1977, well known for their on-stage costumes depicting American cultural stereotypes, as well as their catchy tunes and suggestive lyrics.

The group was the creation of Jacques Morali, a French musical composer. He had written a few dance tunes when he was given a demo tape recorded by singer/actor Victor Willis. Morali approached Willis and told him, "I had a dream that you sang lead on my album and it went very, very big". Willis agreed to sing on the first album, Village People.

It was a success, and demand for live appearances soon followed. Morali and his business partner, Henri Belolo (under the collaboration Can't Stop Productions), hastily built a group of dancers around Willis to perform in clubs and on Dick Clark's American Bandstand. As Village People's popularity grew, Morali, Belolo and Willis saw the need for a permanent "group." They took out an ad in a music trade magazine which read: "Macho Types Wanted: Must Dance And Have A **Moustache**.

MOUSTACHE

A moustache is facial hair grown on the outer surface of the upper lip. It may or may not be accompanied by a beard, hair around the entire face.

The World Beard and Moustache Championships 2007 had 6 sub-categories for moustaches:

Natural – Moustache may be styled without aids.

Mexican – Big and bushy, beginning from the middle of the upper lip and pulled to the side. The hairs are allowed to start growing from up to a maximum of 1.5 cm beyond the end of the upper lip.

Dalí – narrow, long points bent or curved steeply upward; areas past the corner of the mouth must be shaved. Artificial styling aids needed. Named after Salvador Dalí.

English – narrow, beginning at the middle of the upper lip the whiskers are very long and pulled to the side, slightly curled; the ends are pointed slightly upward; areas past the corner of the mouth usually shaved. Artificial styling may be needed.

Imperial – whiskers growing from both the upper lip and cheeks, curled upward (distinct from the royale, or impériale)

Freestyle – All moustaches that do not match other classes. The hairs are allowed to start growing from up to a maximum of 1.5 cm beyond the end of the upper lip. Aids are allowed.

Other types of moustache include:

Fu Manchu – long, downward pointing ends, generally beyond the chin;

'Pancho Villa' moustache – similar to the Fu Manchu but thicker; also known as a "droopy moustache", generally much more so than that normally worn by the historical Pancho Villa.

Handlebar – bushy, with small upward pointing ends. See baseball pitcher Rollie Fingers. Also known as a "spaghetti moustache", because of its stereotypical association with Italian men.

Horseshoe – Often confused with the Fu Manchu style, the horseshoe was possibly popularized by modern cowboys and consists of a full moustache with vertical extensions from the corners of the lips down to the jawline and resembling an upside-down horseshoe. Also known as "biker moustache".

Pencil moustache – narrow, straight and thin as if drawn on by a pencil, closely clipped, outlining the upper lip, with a wide shaven gap between the nose and moustache, widely recognized as being the moustache of choice for the fictional character Gomez Addams in the 1990s series of films based on The Addams Family. Also known as a Mouth-brow, worn by John Waters, Sean Penn and Chris Cornell.

Chevron – thick and wide, usually covering the top of the upper lip. Comedian Jeff Foxworthy and NASCAR driver Richard Petty wear Chevrons.

Toothbrush – thick, but shaved except for about an inch (2.5 cm) in the center; associated with Adolf Hitler, Charlie Chaplin, Oliver Hardy and Michael Jordan in his commercials for Hanes.

Walrus – bushy, hanging down over the lips, often entirely covering the mouth. Worn by John Bolton, Dick Strawbridge, and **Wilford Brimley.**

THIRTEENTH CHAPTER

I've started drinking milk, and Frank is still missing. But let's begin with the milk.

I look out my window one Saturday and happen to spot my neighbor walking up to a dingy white van and handing someone money through the open passenger-side window. Seconds later the side door slides open, my neighbor is handed two large plastic jugs, and the van speeds off. My neighbor is a thirtysomething single mom, one of thousands who got screwed both literally and physically by the guy we all looked up to in kindergarten, feared in high school, and had forgotten even existed in college, a place he only came close to when driving by in his hotwired car after busting up beer joints with his chronically scarred fists. However bad I feel for her, I am careful not to engage in conversation. Sandra is a chatter assassin, a preying hyena waiting patiently for her next unsuspecting victim to cross her path, whereupon she will pounce on and kill it with a never-ending stream of words. *Even her jaws are like that of a hyena,* I think as she opens the door, chewing, a half-eaten sandwich in one hand, a half-baked person in the other. I cut to the chase and throw her a bone of confusion for good measure. "Sandra, that's just awful about Miss Hardgrave. Oh, didn't you hear? She had her purse snatched. By the way, I saw you by the van today."

You know how they say that white is the new black, or sometimes grey is the new black, or even black is the new black? Well, it turns out that milk is the new pot. That is, unpasteurized milk. You sign up online, and once you have gotten clearance to join this underground farming society, sort of the Robin Hood of dairies, you can get in on the goodies. Once a week the trucks roll in – Sandra didn't know from where, but I'd like to think from some *X-Files* utopia where mountain brooks are cool and clear and the sloping pastures thick and green – and when they pass through your area you simply stand on the street corner, give them the cash in exchange for the milk, and off they go. Boom! A simple transaction where nobody gets hurt. I got hold of my first delivery yesterday, and I've gotta say, it's some potent shit. I fill a glass to the brim and watch the light foam set before I pick it up. It's a sensation both cool and smooth, and the milk settles calmly in my stomach. It settles *me* calmly. After a glass I'm not really worried about Frank any more. He's a big guy, no pun intended, and I'm sure he will show up eventually. But just to make sure I call the farm again and ask if they've seen him before I head into work, but it's a negative.

When I arrive at the office I am reminded of the check-up Bri asked me to do as I see her passing through the hall with Pimple Face. If there's one thing that I've got going for myself, apart from my dashing good looks, my witty sense of humor, my magnificent personality, and my ever-evolving sparkling style, it's the appearance that I give a shit about my job. That somehow the laborer's angel has bestowed on me this… let's call it a quality, but it is really more of a grace, is a mystery to me, but as they say, the big crooks always get away clean, it's the small fish that fry. That, and Bri has been so busy with the hacking intrusion that she's probably forgotten about the whole thing. I decide to fix it right away, to show my true-blue colors, and I fetch the paper from my drawer. I unfold it and read the text and I nearly shit a brick. Hell, if my asshole was only big enough I'd shit an entire brick house. The perpetrator is moi. I have been asked by Bri to check up on my own anonymous profile, the one I so self-destructively used to message her. Apparently she swallowed my hook. That's the pitfall of being too good at what you do, even if you hate it. I quickly go on the defensive and take charge of the situation. I need to fix this right away. I put the paper in the trash and pretend I never got it. Moments before I start forgetting, but before I can pretend I never got it, I pick it up, and tear it to little pieces. Then I begin pretending. Then I log on and quickly delete my profile. I have enough dating contacts to take me all the way to the end. Processing, processing, there, I am in the clear. No fingerprints to dust, not a trace to follow.

My job flows a lot easier now that I have set myself a deadline. There are only two women left to scrutinize, and if she isn't among them I lose a job. When I think of it, it's really a win–lose situation, or a lose–win situation, depending on how I look at it. I lose the girl, I lose my job, but I win my freedom. I win the girl and win love, but lose my freedom. Always something sweet with the sour. Never cheese *and* peas. That's why my conscience does not beckon me to continue producing online sludge when the square maiden Diane illuminates my screen.

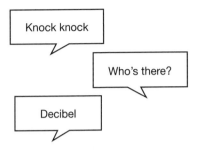

Diane's link-leaping has brought her to units, the glue of our existence, if you think of it. We describe everything in units: it's this far to the grocery store, but only if you go this fast. My pecker is this long, and how much did you say those two hours cost? Units, everything is units. Diane's favorite unit is decibel, partly because it sounds like a name, like Isabel, but mostly because she thinks it's nice to say. "I hear you," I say, "no matter how quiet you say it." She asks about my favorite, and I have to give it some thought. Dollar is a good one but it's too evil, there's too much blood on it. I try to think of some old ones, like fathom – in a fathom deep – and it's cool for obvious reasons but doesn't cut it for number one. I have a thing for light-year because it seems infinite and safe, but it's not infinite, is it? It's over in the blink of a flashlight. Then I hover on fortnight for a bit, fourteen days, but leave it to seek greener pastures elsewhere. A city block appeals to me because it's familiar and very easy to picture. Jiffy is fun to say and has a real-world connection, although it is a bit misleading because nobody, not even Superman, can do anything in 0.01 seconds. One that really gets me is dog year. Maybe that's because I like all expressions that include the word *dog*, like a dog-and-pony show, the top dog, dog-eared, and it's a dog-eat-dog world, but when I think of dogs aging seven years in only one it depresses me, and I continue my search for the perfect unit.

Eventually I have it: Scoville. The Scoville scale is the measurement of the spicy heat in chili peppers, and I think the scale can be directly translated to our own measly lives. At 0 there's no significant heat: we are simply babies in packages. From there on the heat increases for every year, or unit on the scale, until eventually it gets so spicy our eyes water and we burst into flames.

I continue to try Frank's phone at even intervals but with no luck. I imagine him kidnapped: perhaps someone mistook him for a child, and when they discovered that their treasure was a hairy-bodied freak show they freaked and buried him in a swamp, without even having to dig very deep. I decide to go by the bar on my way home and ask for him there. The rest of the day I keep my head down and manage to get by without Bri spotting me. Not that I even remember why I'm staying out of her way, but it seems like the wise thing to do.

Nobody at the bar has seen Frank, and I'm pretty sure the girl behind the counter winks at me. I don't know what that means in dwarf language, maybe You're hot, but it could also mean I want to try to kick your ass, so I get out of there. I consider searching the streets but realize it's ridiculous, we were a hundred miles away. Even so, I can't help but scan each alley on my way home.

At work today I feel all loose and spontaneous; I think it's the raw milk. It soothes my nerves and chills my thoughts, and despite my missing half pint of a compadre I book a ticket to go see my friend Peter in Miami. I really need a change of scenery. Peter is a computer greak-freak and why he lives in Miami when he might as well live in Utah I can't say – a computer screen inside an apartment looks the same everywhere, and Peter isn't one for sunbathing or rumming and coling it with the Cuban *mamacitas*. Nevertheless, we always have a riot when we meet, bracelet buddies since school as we are. I do feel bad about leaving Frank high and dry, wherever it is that he is, but I have my phone and I've left messages everywhere I can think of, and if I think of it anymore I'm afraid my mind will only conjure up the worst possible scenarios. So I take a cab to JFK, and the whole process of checking in, going through security, and everything that is usually such a drag is for once problem-free. Clean as a whistle and smooth as a baby's butt I glide through everything, almost as though the trip *wants* me to be there. I get the emergency seat – I never get the emergency seat, despite my gangly build – and to round things off there's an empty seat between me and the girl by the window. We take off, and I think only good thoughts for a) I think God would rather take down a plane where there are more bad thoughts than one in which people think good things, and b) I don't believe in God but I believe in the inner life of machinery, our metallic children, and that any miracles that happen or don't happen are the product of electric currents, in other words thoughts, and such do I send off big-time into the entire structure of the plane.

Once we buzz along safely above the clouds, I relax enough to take a look around. The girl by the window is actually quite cute. She has a perky little nose, big, white front teeth, bunny-style, and golden plaited hair. I want to hey-how-you-doin' in an original way, but all I can think of is the obvious. "So, you are going to Miami?" Duh. Someone please shoot me. *I'm just kidding, plane, I don't want to die.*

Her name would make a porn star jealous: Honey Golden. She is originally from London, UK (her accent being one of her great assets, the way she draws out each word – oreeallyy – delicately and precisely, and the way peculiar words slip innocently into an ordinary conversation – argy-bargy, bollocks, cheeky bugger, and taking a piss), and we hit it off from the start. We talk about all sorts of things: her life, my life, other people's lives. I lean slightly into the empty seat between us, she does the same from her side, and soon we have inched our bodies close enough to meet in the middle. There she leans her head on my shoulder, and I simply have to turn my hand a quarter lap and lay it on hers. It's a bit of magic at 30,000 feet. It all happens during a movie that we agree to watch simultaneously. We press play at exactly the right time, "Do we press it on three or after three?" I ask, and she says on three, which makes sense, and our two screens sync perfectly. Then her head touches my shoulder and my hand her hand, without my understanding of how it happened. Perhaps it's the altitude: we are closer to space up here, further from the shackles of earth, our blood thinner, our cells panting for air. When someone looking a lot like Joaquin Phoenix is about to shoot someone who is most definitely Mark Wahlberg, or the other way around, we both turn our heads at the same time and have no choice but to kiss. First it's a shy kiss, then it's a friendly kiss, then it comes alive and becomes passionate, and soon my hand is under the blanket and caressing her thigh while we each try to swallow as much of the other's saliva as possible. It's a time lapse, our kissing, because before I know it the bell chimes and the sign lights up that it's seatbelt time and the weather in Miami is sunny and blah blah, *Of course it is, it's Miami,* I think, and Honey Golden and I sit up straight, fix our hair, straighten out anything unhinged, and we begin our the descent.

We wait for the bags together, standing by the carousel without knowing if we can touch each other again now that we are on the ground, our blood thickened and the oxygen level back to normal. Her bag arrives, and directly behind it – a good omen, I think – comes mine. Pure as the polished corners of the temple, that was her London all-girl school's motto. It reverberates in my mind as we walk out together, and the Miami heat slaps us both in the face with a sweaty palm when we leave the air-conditioned terminal. I am about to suggest we share a cab, even though

I don't know where she's going – all I know is that wherever it is, I want to go there also. But kick me in the balls and play "Jingle Bells," suddenly a Dapper Dan kind of fellow with black slick hair, wearing moccasins with no socks, comes up and kisses Honey right on the lips. Kick me again in the balls, this time with razorblade stilettos, when she kisses him back and then removes her tongue from his mouth, turns to me with a smile and says, "This is my fiancé, Caaarloooss."

I take a cab to Peter's and sweat about half my body weight onto the floor as I climb the five stories, only to knock on a door that remains closed and unresponsive no matter how hard I pound it. After five minutes my knuckles start to get raw, and the door on the other side of the corridor opens. Peter is at Comic-Con in San Diego, an Asian guy with freckles offers me, and I've never seen an Asian guy with freckles before, so naturally I am startled and don't think of asking anything about Peter before he closes the door. It doesn't matter. I am drained in the heat and tired of Miami already. I wish Peter would just move to Utah, and without giving it another thought I slither back down the stairs, get in the same cab that brought me here, and return to the airport. There's a flight back the same evening, only this time the aviation spirits are no longer pampering me. It takes me hours of standing in line, talking to one suited dummy after another, and I am nothing short of amazed that I manage to get through security without being zapped with a cattle prod. The flight home is identical to the one I took to get down, except there is no kissing and no movie, and a huge Samoan with forearms the size of my thighs takes the armrest and a good part of my seat space hostage for the duration of the flight.

Today I'm in a brooding mood because I am debating with myself whether Honey is the second or third, or if I should just consider her a fluke of nature. On the one hand, I don't think I should count her because we never dated; on the other hand, part of me wants to get it over and done with, like a serial killer flushing bits and pieces of his victim down the toilet, knowing that one day the pipes will clog and he will be found out, and yet unable to stop flushing. I finally decide that she was indeed a date. I wooed her and we dined – on a plastic tray, but still – and we kissed and dashed and I will never hear from her again. How can it not be a date? Consequently, I now only have one silver bullet left to kill the werewolf of love. It's time to get scientific.

I get out the compiled list of my perfect woman, and I go through it thoroughly. If I am to stand any chance against chance, I need to make the last one fit, snug as a bug, with everything on my list. Here we go.

1. A redhead. Redheads are fierce and mysterious fawns with pale complexions and freckles. They have a mutated gene that sets them apart from all other women in the monochrome world, and this puts them on the threshold of the unknown. Redheads are highly sexed and mischievous. They are fire, passion, earth, blood, and combusting love.

2. Lips. The soft, protruding organ at the mouth, the true eyes of a woman, an instrument so sensitive it can taste, smell, feel, sound, nibble, and grimace all the world's secrets. Truths are told from lips; the deepest broodings are revealed by these blood-filled membranes, and all comfort falls first from the lips of a woman.

3. Hands. The "prehensile, multi-fingered extremities located at the end of an arm" are the tentacles of humans, the eyes with which we feel, the eyes without which there would exist no

shape and form. Hands with long, slender fingers, crisscrossed by bluish veins, and with their own personalities, not fidgeting and nervous, but uncertain and carefully treading. The right type of hand resting in a lap or touching a seat rest briefly as it moves back in the bus is an almost religious revelation.

4. Laughter. When the epiglottis constricts the larynx, the result can be boisterous and alarming, attracting everyone's attention. But I'd rather have it exploding like five-cent firecrackers held in a tightly closed mouth. The laughter that peals out one pearl at the time, as if unstoppable, a surprise even to the person emitting it, is the most sought-after.

5. Voice. For the voice to be born the lungs "must produce adequate airflow and air pressure to vibrate vocal folds"; then all that can be heard can be heard. Most have a voice like stone, and angels sing as if words were made of glass. You can't see on a woman what her voice will be like. It is a test that must speak to pass. When she does, all other sounds drop dead.

6. Eyes. These organs that "detect light and covert it to electro-chemical impulses in neurons," they are all so alike, yet some seem so far from the others. Proper eyes are the hands of a woman, capable of draping, caressing, even slapping a face from afar. An enigma, the seeing is done when the lids are shut, revealing the world within us all.

I take the list and compare it to viable candidates I have saved from the site. Of course voice and laughter are impossible to tell, but it doesn't matter, for I can't even find the red hair, the lips, the hands, and the eyes. I give it a rest for a second and call the police. Not the police of love but the real police. I've put it off for as long as I can now. It's time I report Frank missing. "In the maze, sir?" I don't get the question and ask the female voice on the other end of the line to clarify. "What?" She sounds tired and disinterested in just about everything I tell her. "Did you lose your friend in the maze or outside the maze, sir?" "In the maze, we were in the maze." I say. The voice seems to think about this, just for a second. I can hear it chugging. Then it says, "It seems your friend might still be lost in the maze." "Huh?" That's my reply, "huh?" The voice knows she is right, that she has solved the case of the missing maze man. "Your friend, perhaps he is just lost in the maze. I mean, that is the purpose of them." Perhaps she wasn't there the day they taught the Serve part of Serve and Protect. "For six days!" I want to scream so hard into her headset that her brain pops out her opposite ear. "Ma'am, it was six days ago. I don't think anyone would be lost in the maze for six days," I say calmly. I hear the her think again, and before she can give me another Columbo theory I ask if I can please speak to a detective. That seems to do the trick. I leave descriptions of Frank and the maze, and we hang up.

The thing about days is, you never know whether they are special before they have actually taken place.

I wake up and it feels like any other day: the sun rises, the day breaks, my alarm clock goes off, and I wake up. From my bed I walk through the hallway to the kitchen wearing my soft down slippers – in the mornings I can't stand the harshness of the floor directly against my feet, just as I can't stand the harshness of the world and squint my eyes. I need, for a few waking moments, to be pampered, covered in softness, just like a baby bird rolling around on a mound of its mother's cast-off feathers. Coffee is no friend of mine, but raw milk is, and I sit by the table drinking glass after glass until the floating marker within me has reached proper levels. I am just like Leon, the lonesome assassin (assassins usually are) who meets a coltish Natalie Portman and is lonesome no more. Leon kills like LeBron plays basketball, effective and definite; he drinks milk, he's got a single plant that he cares for as if it were a cat, and had there only been down slippers in the set wardrobe, I am sure he would have used those too. So I am Leon, and I take a shower, get dressed, and sit on the subway, where nobody notices me.

At work Pimple Face and his minions have cleared the premises, and the sordid calm that once hung so thick between our heads and the inner ceiling has returned. I feel like gnawing my fingers off. I always do the moment before I begin, the big maestro by his piano, and when I finally join the silent clatter of keyboard symphonies I am so over Leon.

Three things happen, each harmless enough by itself, but when they come together they form a devastating occurrence. Why always three? You may ask yourself this. Let's see, there were the three wise men, the three little piggies, the Three Stooges, the Three Musketeers, the Three Tenors and the Three Amigos ("Time for plan B. Plan A was to break into El Guapo's fortress." "And that you have done, now what?" "Well we really don't have a plan B. We didn't expect for the first plan to work. Sometimes you can overplan these things."). Three is the first odd prime number and the second smallest prime; it is both the first Fermat prime ($22n + 1$) and the first Mersenne prime ($2n - 1$), as well as the first lucky prime. However, it's the second Sophie Germain prime, the second Mersenne prime exponent, the second factorial prime ($2! + 1$), the second Lucas prime, the second Stern prime. Three is the first unique prime due to the properties of its reciprocal. Three is the aliquot sum of 4. Three is the third Heegner number. Three is the second triangular number, and it is the only prime triangular number. Three is the only prime that is one less than a perfect square. Any other number that is $n2 - 1$ for some integer n is not prime, since it is $(n - 1)(n + 1)$. This is true for 3 as well, but in its case one of the factors is 1. Three non-collinear points determine a plane and a circle. Three is the fifth Fibonacci number and the third that is unique. In the Perrin sequence, however, 3 is both the zeroth and third Perrin number. Three is the fourth open meandric number. It seems three is also the magic number, the figure that rocks our world. But until it does I work away – *merrily* would be an overstatement, but I swallow my bile and get on with it. Up to here nothing points towards this day being special, out of the ordinary. The day I meet the one.

It is around three (three again!) in the afternoon. I am fidgeting with an ad while trying to choose my last date. One third of my mind is thinking about what I will do when I quit my job – when, for at this stage I don't think that my last date will present herself as the savior I have desired. Half of that third – that would be one-sixth of my total brainpower – can't stop thinking that I'll end up on the street, and it keeps flashing pictures of gutters flooded with rainwater and my tufted body sprawled out on the sidewalk. The other half of the third, so another sixth, goes through the options as if going through a catalog in alphabetical order: accountant, abbot, acrobat, aerospace engineer, alchemist (What you studying? How to make gold.), alligator wrestler (We lost another two students yesterday, damn those snappy reptiles!), anger management counselor (You shut the fuck up and control your anger, faggot face!), ant farmer (Let's see now, that's Peter and that's Terence, and that's John, and that's Cecilia, and that's Debra, and, no wait, that's not Debra that's Stewart, and that's…), apple picker (One apple sat on the tree; it fell to the ground, and now one apple fell to the ground.), archer, Avon lady, and so forth. Of the second third of my brain, about ten percent is thinking about Frank and a whopping 90 percent about my extraterrestrial ex-girlfriend. That 90 percent is in turn divided into smaller packages dealing with specific issues: jealousy, resentment, good memories, longing, hate, etc. The final third of my brain is occupied with sex. In that space vaginas, tits, lips, boobs, asses, and collarbones float constantly like balloons captured in a room.

So here I sit, my brain computing on so many different levels it is nearly glowing red hot, when number one and number two happen. First my phone rings, and at the moment I pick it up a familiar character appears in the opening to my prism. The voice from the phone emits word after word; I hear each of them, but since there is literally no space left inside my head the best I can do is to repeat them. "We think the big book about little people is a great idea, and we'd like you to come in and talk about the contract." As I mouth the words, Frank wiggles his eyebrows at me, waggles them right up and down a few times, as if he was exercising, while pulling a woman into sight. He lifts his hand and twinkles his fingers back and forth, also as if he was exercising them, and I keep repeating every word the voice on the other end of the line emits. I see a ring on Frank's finger, and the woman at his side, round and earthy with very clear, round eyes, blushes and huddles up closer to him, and in the middle of all these goings-on, as if two things were not enough, the third comes up behind Frank and his fiancée, excuses herself, and steps past them and into my prism. Bri moves her lips, but the only thing I can hear is the voice on the other end of the receiver. "Yes," I say, "yes." It comes from deep within, an automated response, a reptile reflex designed to save my ass from conundrums like this, and when the phone goes dead I can finally hear what Bri is saying and while Frank winks his eyebrows and twinkles his fingers, I don't think, I merely answer, and the answer is yes, I have checked out the profile and it belongs to me. I sent you those messages.

It's awkward moments for everyone. Frank is the one to break the silence with a tactful cough. This shakes Bri from her frozen pose, and she snaps her mouth shut and walks out of my prism. I'm not sure what I'm feeling. Frank and Moira – that's her name, Moira – step inside, and they are so short nobody on the outside can actually see them standing there. I am frazzled and know not what to say, so that's what I point out, that nobody can see them there, but they don't mind, everything just seems to ease off them, the way nothing sticks to love. Frank goes first. He tells me about how when he walked around the maze, roughly fifty yards in, he turned into what he thought was part of the maze, but it was really only a wider row of cornstalks. He followed it straight for a long time, with nothing to see other than the cornstalks in front of his face, the dirt at his feet and the glimpses of sky above. He walked for what felt like hours, and when he finally came to the end of the cornfield he crossed a road and continued into the next field, this one filled with pumpkins – big, orange pumpkins larger than his own body – and he walked across this field for hours until finally the sky grew dark and the rain began to fall. By then he was tired and cold, but he was in the middle of nowhere and all he had on him was his Swiss Army knife, so he walked up to the biggest pumpkin he could find, carved out a hole big enough for his shoulders and hips to squeeze through, emptied it of seeds and stringy meat, and crawled inside, just in time for the rain to start pouring. All night he sat in the pumpkin, sometimes sleeping, sometimes lying awake and listening to the rain tapping the hollow pumpkin from above. It sounded like being inside a drum, he said. Early next morning, as the sun rose over the field, he crawled outside and brushed the pumpkin debris off his clothes, but still it looked like he had been born out of the pumpkin and was covered in some of the placenta. Again he began walking, unsure of which way he had come the day before, but he chose a path that seemed easy to walk and trotted on.

By midday he became very thirsty, and by late afternoon he was starving. But the end of the field was nowhere in sight, at least not from where he was standing. He began looking for another pumpkin to house him for the night, and when he found one that looked pleasant he carved a hole and scraped out the innards, but not as carefully as the day before, and crawled inside. During the night there was no rain, and he fell into a deep sleep. He awoke feeling that the whole world was spinning. *I am dying of thirst and hunger,* he thought, *this is how it begins, the end.* But when he regained consciousness he noticed that it wasn't his head that was spinning, it was the pumpkin itself. The pumpkin had been hoisted up on the back of a truck that huffed and puffed across the field. When it stopped he climbed out, and there, from the passenger-side door, out jumped Moira.

They got engaged that same evening, in the candlelight on the second floor in the barn, and they ate pumpkin pie and toasted with pumpkin wine. Frank finishes the story by again twinkling his fingers, sending sparkles flying from the ring, and waggles his eyebrows up and down. When they leave a small part of my brainpower is released, the ten percent of the one third, and right about then I understand what has happened. Bri knows it was me who sent the messages to her profile. I will lose my job. And the book, they want to publish the book so everything may be okay after all. *I'll have to ask for an advance to tide me over until fame and fortune arrives,* I think. With quiet resignation, and lots of relief, I tidy up my desk and put the few things I want to save into an empty shoebox. When I'm done I take down the poster of Amadeus and roll it up, then tuck it under my arm. Mona Lisa I leave behind. Belongings in hand, I begin the walk towards Bri's office, trying to prepare an appropriate goodbye, but by the time I get there I have come up with nothing. I knock on her door and open it without waiting for a reply. "Listen," I say, "I'll be on my way. You can keep *Mona Lisa* and…"

"Do you really want to go on a date with me?" Her voice interrupts me, but it is not what she says, it's the way it sounds as she says it. It's the voice of an angel, and all other sounds run and hide in shame as it enters the scene. "I mean, if you do, I'd like for us to go on a date." I watch her lips as she speaks, unable to move. They seem to be alive in her face, not even part of her face but a creature of their own. The slight curvature, the form that I am sure is able to take the whole world between its cushions and carry it onward forever. I drop the poster, and it unrolls face-up on Bri's office floor. Tom Dulce is laughing like a hyena. Bri looks at the poster and lets out a pearly marvel of laughter, a tiny explosion in her mouth. "I always meant to tell you, I love that movie." I am dumbstruck – I probably look as much – and she points to the poster. Long, slender fingers, crisscrossed by bluish veins, uncertain and delicate, just the right type of hand. I notice her hair – how haven't I given any weight to the fact that her hair is golden red, a copper-tinted shiny ball of fur fire? "So, what do you say? Is it a date then?" Her eyes drape my face and direct my gaze into hers. It's a firm grip that heats my skin and causes it to bubble. I have been blind and now I can see. It was her, all along it was her.

FOURTEENTH CHAPTER

I go back to my desk and reinstate myself. I unpack the shoebox, but as I'm about to put up the poster of Tom Dulce as Amadeus I realize it is still in Bri's office. As chance would have it, I retrieve it later that evening when we meet at Cipriani. But before I know anything about that I have once again pulled out my presentation pad and run through the motions of meeting with my starry-eyed students.

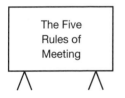

The Five
Rules of
Meeting

NUMBER ONE – NOTHING SAYS "I LOVE YOU" LIKE FLOWERS
And although you want to avoid those three little words like the plague, a bouquet of roses sends the signal that you are taking it seriously enough. Also, red is the color of blood, and blood is what you are trying to make boil.

NUMBER TWO – DRESS FOR SUCCESS

There are occasions when shorts and a soggy T-shirt with a memory pattern of stains may well be appropriate, but no matter what they say, women tend to be drawn to the materialistic side of life, the caveman provider-and-protector syndrome, and the right outfit will convey just that.

NUMBER THREE – GROOMING TO IMPRESS

Your mother should already have taught you this, but in case you were out roaming the neighborhood sidewalks on your Big Wheels when these life wisdoms were imparted, here is a recap. Shower. And brush your teeth – one misplaced blade of parsley can seriously damage your reputation.

NUMBER FOUR – DON'T BE A WEIRDO

If you don't know what this means, you are probably already a weirdo and your chances are slim to nil. Hints: party tricks, practical jokes, and a generally insane personality should be avoided.

NUMBER FIVE – HAVE SOME FUCKING INTEGRITY

This means holding off on the sucking up. It can be hard for men when faced with a beautiful woman. Men are genetically programmed to try to impress women in order to have them. Through the ages this has taken different routes, from killing the less agile male specimens with a club to talking about your car or the models you've dated. It's worth saying again: have some fucking integrity, man.

The Amadeus poster has been framed, and it sticks up from behind the table at which Bri is already sitting. Everything moves quickly now. Bri hands me the framed poster; we sit, and words and glances are tossed back and forth between us, food is brought in and empty plates brought out, wineglasses are constantly half-full. She's not the Bri I know, the one I didn't know. I always figured she was tough-skinned, with razor-sharp elbows, but the impression I get as the evening lulls forward to a standstill – the bubble has descended and surrounds our entire table – is of a sensitive, loving, and thoughtful woman with a thing for poodles. Yet I've never seen her with a single poodle, and that's her in a nutshell, an enigma. The evening progresses, unfolding over a timeless landscape, while our hands are drawn closer and closer over the table until they finally touch. Like two shy animals they perform a greeting ritual involving finger-probing and delicate maneuvers to win the other hand's confidence. This is the first time we have touched, I think, since the day I started and we shook hands. Bri's eyes glow along with her radiant hair, which threatens to set the restaurant ablaze. Our hands entwine, and the waiters, having the sense to sense the shift in atmosphere, stay clear of the eye of the storm. It's hard to say what is in the kiss. It's passionate and alluring, but the message eludes me. Only to Bri does the message seem clear. "Move in with me," she says, and I think, *Why not? We already have a framed poster.*

As it turns out, that is all the furniture I bring with me. I box up my old things – it takes a week, working at supersonic speeds – and just like that, brush my hands, my old life is gone. I walk through the empty rooms one last time – it smells of me and it smells of her – then I take a cab with two suitcases filled with clothes, my five favorite books and movies, and I arrive in a new life. My poster is already in place. It hangs in the laundry room above the ironing board. We spend the evening in bed, a giant behemoth of a bed, bigger than a minivan, but Bri still lies straight as a plank on her side. We make love, and it's the same as the kiss, passionate on the surface, but the deeper meaning does not yet dare come out of hiding. It's all so new. We are a coat of freshly applied paint, racing to dry. The next day Bri heads into work early, but we have breakfast together. Bri drinks her coffee while I only sit with my cup, feeling the warm steam rise into my bathrobe. The view from the kitchen table is amazing. Solid glass windows, from floor to ceiling, open up to the New York morning. A flower stands in a vase in the middle of the table; there's British lemon curd, bread baked with artesian water, Swiss butter, and freshly squeezed orange juice. It arrives every morning in a box from a delicate deli that caters to the delicately rich. There's a desk with a computer upstairs; Bri thinks it's best if I work from home for a while, to avoid tension at the office. *Home*, I haven't gotten used to that word yet. How could I? It's not even been twenty-four hours. I agree with her, in the way that I just don't have an opinion. I don't care much about my job, but I haven't said as much. There are many things I haven't yet told her. But all in all, I think it's a good idea to work from here.

When Bri leaves, we kiss just like husband and wife. Then I walk around the apartment and snoop. Snooping isn't the best way to describe it, since this is now where I live, but my face is in none of the framed pictures in the living room, nor have I bought any of the books in the bookshelf, and the closet holds only feminine attire. I open drawers and cabinets, I take whiffs of whisky bottles and panties, and I try to piece together a life that belongs to the woman of my dreams. Is this all a dream then? I don't ponder, I simply walk around in my down slippers and Bri's guest bathrobe until I get bored and settle in front of the computer. I have a new message on the intranet. At first it confuses me. Diane would never use such a word. Then I realize it's from Bri.

Hello, darling.

I'm not sure about it. It feels as if I am being unfaithful to Diane. But it agrees with my ego, being called darling after so long. I want to belong to someone. After answering Bri I knock out a few ads before I suddenly feel tired all over again and revert back to bed. I wake up an hour before Bri gets home, and we go out for dinner. Bri seems to have something on her mind. "Something wrong?" I say. She looks at me with the sweetest smile, but her eyes droop slightly as if sadness is weighing them down. "I want to have a baby," she says. We talk about it in the car on the way home and in the elevator up to her apartment – *our* apartment – and by the time we reach bed she has managed to make a convincing point out of a ludicrous suggestion. She is ripe, her seeds are in their prime, going on towards the inevitable rot. It's hard for a career gal, meeting the right man, being there, building a relationship that works in all aspects, and in the event that all goes smoothly, after a few years plan for a baby. "I'm not young anymore," she says, and I do understand – it's like that for women – but the world has been spinning so fast lately I don't know what to make of it. It spins so fast I have to straight-out ask her. "Are you saying you want to have a baby with me?" She snuggles her nose under my chin and purrrrs out a long yeeesss. We make love, and I release my seed in her without thought. Afterward, we lie on our backs, sweating out the remaining heat, and she confuses me and breaks my heart a little. "You don't have to feel you have to take care of it. We can even draw up papers if it makes you feel better." It takes a few days for this to sink in.

Meanwhile we are a regular couple. She goes to work while I'm working from home, going out to dinner, making love, in the manner of those who've been together for years. We've skipped the honeymoon, meshing our two lives together with a zipper instead of a silk thread. Outwardly I am the boyfriend, but inwardly I am in a constant brooding state. Does she only want my sperm, is that what this is? Am I an idiot, or is this what a relationship really is? I got everything on my list. Perhaps it doesn't get better than this? Perhaps life is simply a collection of practicalities, and thinking about it, dreaming about it, is a lot different from actually living it. I try to feel happiness, and it's there at times, poking its bewildered head out. It's the littlest things: her laughter, her skin against mine, how we slide across each other, her high heels in the elevator, the way she steers her car.

Soon she brings it up again. She doesn't want to pressure me, and that's why she suggests we go to a clinic to make a donation. The first thought I have is that we donate money and get a baby, but soon enough I realize that she is talking about my sperm. "That way you don't have to feel pressured, and the doctor can inseminate it when my hormones are just right," she says. It sounds proper, well thought through, and I can't think of a reason to say no. When the day comes, Bri stays home from work and we go to the clinic on Park Avenue. It's an office located at street level, just a small waiting room with some old magazines on a table, not really what I would have expected. Then again, I've never donated sperm before. A doctor with a ponytail greets us. I'm not sure he is a real doctor; he looks more like a scientist to me, with clinical, studying eyes, as if peering through a microscope has permanently changed his view of the world. There are papers to sign and a check to write, and while Bri cuts the check I sign the papers. Bri then waits in the lobby while the doctor/scientist leads me to a darkened room with some porn magazines casually flung on a table and a flat-screen on the wall. I sit back in the La-Z-Boy and use the remote to turn on the TV and hopefully get turned on in the process. It's a strange feeling, knowing your girlfriend and the clinic's crew are waiting outside while you're supposed to jerk off into a plastic receptacle. It's girl-on-girl action, and I fast-forward to a scene where a tight Asian chick is impaled by a black stud. She gets sex sweat on her forehead, and so do I trying to get a rise out of my pecker. I don't fret and watch some more. I get to a scene where a mature-looking farm girl with huge knockers seduces the young farmhand in the barn. He reams her from behind like some stallion, and I stroke my monkey to wake it up, but it seems to be forever asleep. Instead I pick up a magazine where a girl with a ball-gag in her mouth is whipped by a woman wearing a strap-on. The strap-on later goes where it was meant to go, but my willy is still limp as a noodle.

This has never happened before. Being locked in a room filled with a selection of porn for all tastes, sanctioned by my girlfriend, even by a doctor, to medicinally wank off, and I can't get a stiffy? I try standing up to get a better grip, but to no avail. I change DVDs, and the screen soon fills with Hungarian honeys that run a prison camp where everyone is naked, even the guards. I try my best but finally I give up and switch it off. Nothing works, and I've realized why. Something inside me doesn't want me to do this. Perhaps God doesn't want me to stroke one out this way. I'm sure it is against His principles, as the divine creator, to get pregnant by artificial insemination. I look around the room and act fast. There's a bottle of Alcogel and some tissues on the table; I give it a couple of good pumps right down into the receptacle. Looks a lot like goo to me, and I snap the lid shut.

"I'm proud of you," Bri says, "I don't know how to thank you. Let's go out for dinner." Strangely, the bubble still encapsulates us, and at dinner the outside world doesn't exist. It's just the two of us, although Bri's mind seems to be working overtime elsewhere. When we get home she doesn't try to sleep with me, she simply yawns, puts on one of those black eye masks they give you on airplanes, and falls asleep within ten breaths. Eventually I drift off wondering how long it will take before my sperm sample is deemed worthless.

The next morning, Bri heads to the office and I stay in bed until she's gone. I log onto the computer and send Diane a holla. I'm feeling down and need a pick-me-up, but when I don't hear back from her I try to do some ads before I realize the fruitlessness of it. There's an emptiness in Bri's apartment, despite the airy space, polished steel bars and glass walls, and it's creeping inside me. Of course, there are many types of emptiness, some of which are enviable compared to others. Once – it was late in the summer a few years back – I was up in the Adirondacks with some friends, picking our way from campsite to campsite. We had set camp by a lake with an Indian name, I forget which, and surrounding us on all sides was a forest of big, leafy trees with thin trunks. I got up early and felt I had to move or go crazy. So I unzipped the tent, stuck my shoes outside, stepped into them, and took off without waking any of the others. I walked along the lake, through the spaciously set forest where trees were never closer than the length of two men lying down. The ground was covered with a sawdusty dirt that had a slight give, and it shot me onward with each step I took. There were no real paths, but I kept the lake on my right side at all times so as not to get lost. I walked for about an hour; the sun had risen, and already the heat of the day was climbing to rival yesterday's. Drops of sweat ran down my back with feather-light movements, and when I came upon the river I didn't think twice. It flowed from the lake, where to I did not know. Reeds grew along the banks in clusters, but where I stood there was a small clearing where one could easily wade in. I cast off my clothes and left them in a pile on top of my shoes on the riverbank. The water was cool but not cold – at any rate, bearable – and the longer I stood there the less I felt the temperature. I waited until it no longer disturbed my skin and plunged into it. The river was only about thirty feet wide, so when I resurfaced I did so in the middle. The current was weak but persistent; if I had held my breath and floated, the water would have carried me gently downstream, but when I laid flat and took slow, steady strokes, the river held me in one place. It felt like flying.

Without warning it started to rain. Big raindrops, the kind that have collected themselves over hot summer days until near bursting, began to drop from the sky and puckered the surface of the river. Within a minute the water was boiling. I focused on each droplet as it crashed into the water. Immediately after each impact a small plume of water rose into the air, creating another water drop falling, and it another, so in fact each raindrop was perpetually falling into the river. Right then and there, amidst the bombardment of the gently caressing water, I experienced complete emptiness, so vast that if I had sunk right then and there to the bottom of the river I suspect I wouldn't have bothered to come up again.

The emptiness I feel in the empty apartment sitting in front of the computer contains some of the same factors, but if I were to close my eyes and let the apartment take me down to the bottom, if I resigned myself completely, I'm not so sure peace would find me. I try to shake my feelings with some link-leaping.

ALLEN WILFORD BRIMLEY

Allen Wilford Brimley (born September 27, 1934) is an American actor. He has appeared in such films as *The China Syndrome*, *Cocoon*, *The Thing* and *The Firm*. Brimley has also done television commercials, including ads for Quaker Oats and Liberty Medical.

Prior to his career in acting, Brimley worked as a ranch hand, wrangler, blacksmith, and a bodyguard for **Howard Hughes**.

HOWARD HUGHES

Howard Robard Hughes, Jr. (December 24, 1905 – April 5, 1976) was an American business magnate, industrialist, aviator, engineer, film producer, director, hotelier, philanthropist, and was one of the wealthiest people in the world. He gained prominence from the late 1920s as a maverick film producer, making big-budget and often controversial films like *The Racket* (1928), *Hell's Angels* (1930), *Scarface* (1932), and *The Outlaw* (1943).

As early as the 1930s, Hughes displayed signs of mental illness, primarily obsessive-compulsive disorder. Close friends reported that he was obsessed with the size of peas, one of his favorite foods, and used a special fork to sort them by size.

While directing *The Outlaw*, Hughes became fixated on a minor flaw in one of Jane Russell's blouses, claiming that the fabric bunched up along a seam and gave the appearance of two nipples on each breast. He was reportedly so upset by the matter that he wrote a detailed memorandum to the crew on how to fix the problem.

In December 1947, Hughes told his aides that he wanted to screen some movies at a film studio near his home. Hughes stayed in the studio's darkened screening room for more than four months, never leaving. He subsisted exclusively on chocolate bars and milk, and relieved himself in the empty bottles and containers. He was surrounded by dozens of Kleenex boxes, which he continuously stacked and re-arranged.

After the screening room incident, Hughes moved into a bungalow at the Beverly Hills Hotel. He also rented out several other rooms for his aides, his wife, and his numerous girlfriends. His erratic behavior continued, however, as he would sit naked in his bedroom with a pink hotel napkin placed over his genitals, watching movies. In one year, he spent an estimated $11 million at the hotel.

In a bout of obsession with his home state, Hughes began purchasing all restaurant chains and four star hotels that had been founded within the borders of Texas.

The wealthy and aging Howard Hughes, accompanied by his entourage of personal aides, began moving from one hotel to another, always taking up residence in the top floor penthouse. During the last ten years of his life, from 1966 to 1976, Hughes lived in hotels in Beverly Hills, Boston, Las Vegas, Nassau, Freeport, Vancouver, London, Managua, Acapulco, and others.

On November 24, 1966 (Thanksgiving Day), Hughes arrived in Las Vegas by railroad car and moved into the Desert Inn. Because he refused to leave the hotel and to avoid further conflicts with the owners of the hotel, Hughes bought the Desert Inn in early 1967. The hotel's eighth floor became the nerve center of his empire and the ninth-floor penthouse became Hughes' personal residence. He bought the small Silver Slipper casino only to reposition the hotel's trademark neon silver slipper, visible from Hughes bedroom, which apparently had been keeping him up at night.

Hughes was a lifelong aircraft enthusiast and pilot. At Rogers Airport in Los Angeles, he learned to fly from pioneer aviators, including Moye Stephens. He set many world records and commissioned the construction of custom aircraft to be built for himself while heading Hughes Aircraft at the airport in Glendale. Operating from there, the most technologically important aircraft he commissioned was the Hughes H-1 Racer. On September 13, 1935, Hughes, flying the H-1, set the landplane airspeed record of 352 mph (566 km/h) over his test course near Santa Ana, California. A year and a half later, on January 19, 1937, flying a redesigned H-1 Racer featuring extended wings, Hughes set a new transcontinental airspeed record by flying non-stop from Los Angeles to Newark in 7 hours, 28 minutes and 25 seconds (beating his own previous record of 9 hours, 27 minutes). His average ground speed over the flight was 322 mph (518 km/h).

The H-1 Racer was donated to the **Smithsonian** in 1975.

THE SMITHSONIAN

The Smithsonian Institution is an educational and research institute and associated museum complex, administered and funded by the government of the United States and by funds from its endowment, contributions, and profits from its retail operations, concessions, licensing activities, and magazines. The Smithsonian has requested $797.6 million from Congress in 2011 to fund its operations. While most of its 19 museums, its zoo, and its nine research centers facilities are located in Washington, D.C., sites are also located in New York City, Virginia, Panama, and elsewhere. The Smithsonian has over 136 million items in its collections, publishes two magazines named Smithsonian (monthly) and Air & Space (bimonthly), and employs the **Smithsonian Police** to protect visitors, staff, and the property of its museums.

SMITHSONIAN POLICE

The Smithsonian Institution Office of Protection Services is the guard force of the Smithsonian Institution.

It is a federal guard force with limited special police authority tasked with protecting visitors, staff, property, and grounds of the federally-owned and managed Smithsonian Institution museums and research centers in Washington, D.C., New York City and **Virginia**.

VIRGINIA

The Commonwealth of Virginia is a U.S. state on the Atlantic Coast of the Southern United States. Virginia is nicknamed the "Old Dominion" and sometimes the "Mother of Presidents" after the eight U.S. presidents born there.

Virginia has an annual average of 35–45 days of thunderstorm activity, particularly in the western part of the state, and an average annual precipitation of 42.7 inches (1,085 mm). Cold air masses arriving over the mountains in winter can lead to significant snowfalls, such as the Blizzard of 1996 and winter storms of 2009–2010. The interaction of these elements with the state's topography creates distinct microclimates in the Shenandoah Valley, the mountainous southwest, and the coastal plains. Virginia averages seven tornadoes annually, most F2 or lower on the **Fujita scale**.

FUJITA SCALE

The Fujita scale (F-Scale), or Fujita-Pearson scale, is a scale for rating tornado intensity, based primarily on the damage tornadoes inflict on human-built structures and vegetation.

The scale was introduced in 1971 by Tetsuya Fujita of the University of Chicago who developed the scale together with Allen Pearson (path length and width additions in 1973), head of the National Severe Storms Forecast Center (predecessor to the Storm Prediction Center.

The original scale as derived by Fujita was a theoretical 13-level scale (F0–F12) designed to smoothly connect the **Beaufort scale** and the Mach number scale.

BEAUFORT SCALE

The Beaufort Scale is an empirical measure for describing wind speed based mainly on observed sea conditions (on land it is categorized by the physical effects it has on vegetation and structures). Its full name is the Beaufort Wind Force Scale.

The scale was created in 1805 by Sir Francis Beaufort, an Irish-born Royal Navy Officer, while serving on HMS Woolwich. The scale that carries Beaufort's name had a long and complex evolution, from the previous work of others, including **Daniel Defoe** the century before.

DANIEL DEFOE

Daniel Defoe (ca. 1659-1661 – 24 April 1731), born Daniel Foe, was an English writer, journalist, and pamphleteer, who gained fame for his novel *Robinson Crusoe*. Defoe is notable for being one of the earliest proponents of the novel, as he helped to popularize the form in Britain and is among the founders of the **English novel.**

ENGLISH NOVEL

The English novel is an important part of English literature.

The Romantic period saw the first flowering of the English novel. Horace Walpole's 1764 novel, *The Castle of Otranto*, invented the Gothic fiction genre, combining elements of horror and romance. Mary Shelley is best known for her novel *Frankenstein* (1818), infusing elements of the Gothic novel and Romantic movement. Frankenstein's chilling tale suggests modern organ transplants and tissue regeneration, reminding readers of the moral issues raised by today's medicine.

For many years, novels were considered light reading for young, single women. Novels written for this audience were often heavily didactic and, like earlier English literature, attempted to provide examples of correct conduct.

Jane Austen wrote highly polished novels about the life of the landed gentry, seen from a woman's point of view, and wryly focused on practical social issues, especially marriage and money. Austen's *Pride and Prejudice* (1813) is often considered the epitome of the romance genre.

It was in the Victorian era (1837–1901) that the novel became the leading form of literature in English.

Charles Dickens emerged on the literary scene in the 1830s, confirming the trend for serial publication. Dickens wrote vividly about London life and struggles of the poor, in books such as *Oliver Twist*, but in a good-humored fashion, accessible to readers of all classes.

Key to Victorian style is the concept of the intrusive narrator and the address to the reader. For example, the author might interrupt his/her narrative to pass judgment on a character, or pity or praise another, while later seeming to exclaim "Dear Reader!" and inform or remind the reader of some other relevant issue.

In 2003 the BBC carried out a UK survey entitled **The Big Read** in order to find the "nation's best-loved novel" of all time.

THE BIG READ

The Big Read was a survey on books carried out by the BBC in the United Kingdom in 2003, where over three quarters of a million votes were received from the British public to find the nation's best-loved novel of all time. The year-long survey was the biggest single test of public reading taste to date, and culminated with several programmes hosted by celebrities, advocating their favorite books.

The British public voted originally for any novel that they wished. From this, a list of 200 was drawn up, with the highest 21 then put forward for further voting, on the provision that only one book per author was permitted in the top 21.

Top 200 in the United Kingdom

1. *The Lord of the Rings* by J. R. R. Tolkien
2. *Pride and Prejudice* by Jane Austen
3. *His Dark Materials* by Philip Pullman
4. *The Hitchhiker's Guide to the Galaxy* by Douglas Adams
5. *Harry Potter and the Goblet of Fire* by J. K. Rowling
6. *To Kill a Mockingbird* by Harper Lee
7. *Winnie-the-Pooh* by A. A. Milne
8. *Nineteen Eighty-Four* by George Orwell
9. *The Lion, the Witch and the Wardrobe* by C. S. Lewis
10. *Jane Eyre* by Charlotte Brontë
11. *Catch-22* by Joseph Heller

12. *Wuthering Heights* by Emily Brontë
13. *Birdsong* by Sebastian Faulks
14. *Rebecca* by Daphne du Maurier
15. *The Catcher in the Rye* by J. D. Salinger

I stop right there, fourteen steps from the top. My heart reverberates in the silence. I know instinctively that it means something. It must mean something. Perhaps the time has come to tie off the bag? The publication of my first book has been put on hold because of the lawsuit. It's been a roller coaster of emotions and paper, a dreary and at times sleep-inducing roller coaster, but still a ride with harrowing bends and free-falls. We've been caught in this limbo for several months since the holy Salinger's passing, and without thinking about what or why I pick up the phone. *I need to do this,* I think as the secretary puts me on hold. It has to mean something.

My lawyers arrange a meeting already the next day, and I dust off my old school blazer. The son is there and one lawyer, two lawyers, three lawyers, just like the first time. We sit, on each side of a long conference table, and although we've already met, this disease of the corporate world spread by the paper mafia, business cards slide across the table from all directions. I don't have one to slide but nevertheless receive two. After a few pleasantries exchanged between the lawyers, shop talk, it takes a turn for the worse. Perhaps the words are, *You ruined the last six months of my father's life,* but all I hear is: *You killed my father.* Lawyers hawk and shuffle paper, waiting for my reply, but what is there to say that would change anything, that would make it all better? *Yes, but he was so old and would have soon expired anyway* doesn't quite cut it, so I keep my mouth shut and wonder when the sign will show itself. Surely it must have meant something that my link-leaping led me here? Events must come attached to some sort of...well, purpose? *We can change the title,* one lawyer says to another, *and call Phoebe something else, and what if...* I zone out. I've heard it all before, the compromising, the chopping up until nothing is left but a mauled carcass nobody wants to come near. It was a mistake coming here. I play with my business cards and wait for it all to end. I balance them on end and build a fort that is really nothing more than an upside-down *V.* It balances delicately in the midst of chaos. Suddenly Salinger's son sneezes, and the expelled air pummels my house to the ground. It doesn't face me. I can't be faced. I simply just move my focus from the wreckage, the two now flat pieces of paper, to the meticulously printed text on them. I jump-skip over each letter, making each card last for minutes. In the midst of this almost lucid concentration my mind is momentarily freed from thoughts about my job, my ex-girlfriend, even sex, and I experience a gap with clarity of thought. Two words stand out, ten letters, five per word. This is the message. All around me talk is talked, I am somehow involved, but before me lies the unlocked door. The tree has spoken. I excuse myself under my breath and rush out of the conference room, through the office hallway to the elevator, and all the way down to the ground I can't stop myself from repeating her name, Diane Coney, Diane Coney, Diane Coney.

I rush back to the apartment and dive down in front of the computer. She has to be there, she has to.

Diane!
Are you there?

Seconds move like seconds, but each carries an indefinite pause before tripping over the edge. The soft humming from the building holds me suspended in the moment. Finally her rectangle appears.

I am here.

I want to tell her so many things – my mind is bubbling with words and feelings – but right now I stick to the bare essentials.

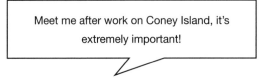

Meet me after work on Coney Island, it's extremely important!

I am alive and I know exactly what I'm doing. I pack my not-yet-unpacked bags and drag them to the front door. Something, I'm forgetting something. I have to tell Bri. I stand over the notepad in the kitchen, ready to scribble down my message. It's been fun? No, it hasn't. She just used me to get a baby. There was no love there, only cool calculation. She is sharp-elbowed after all. *I know you were only after my fertilizer, sorry the test tube is filled with sanitizer. PS. I quit, thank god and hallelujah.* I have no idea why I rhyme, it just comes out that way. Back by the door I still feel like I'm forgetting something.

With the frame tucked under my arm, I decide to leave my bags behind. Casualties of the war of love, although there was none of either. Nevertheless, I don't feel like lugging them around right now. I'm in a hurry to see the girl of my dreams. Why not? It's not crazy when you think of it. All this time she's been right there, under my nose. The perfect one. We have the same interests, the same sense of humor, we get each other. It doesn't matter what she looks like, the list was a stupid, shallow thing to do, a product of the increasingly artificial world I live in. I wanted the details to be perfect, the finish to glow, but I forgot about substance. My list is a list of hollowness, my own perhaps, projected upon a fantasy creation that was meant to save me. I've been nothing but a damned fool.

I hurry down the subway with my framed poster and I feel like laughing, just like Amadeus laughed, and I let one rip. People look at me, but guess what, I don't give a fuck. I have found my integrity. J. D. Salinger and his holy ghost, thank you very much.

It's different this time, the ride to Coney Island. I feel this is where it all started. I suppose it all really started when dust particles collided deep in outer space a billion years ago, but look where it's taken us: it's fantastic. There's subway trains, Ferris wheels, neon signs, seagulls, candied apples, hot dogs, gum on the sidewalk, and the endless ocean. I walk down the steps and sit on a bench right opposite the entrance. It's a gloomy day, weatherwise, but it doesn't matter. Nothing matters. Only that I get a chance to tell Diane how I feel. I watch people come and go, couples with kids, couples without, groups of youngsters hoping something will simply happen. The Land without Shadows, the Native Americans called it, and I suppose I can see where that came from, its compass orientation keeping the beach area in sunlight all day, which would be true if not for the clouds. Shadows do however fall, I notice, behind parked cars, from the backsides of the wooden shacks that house ball-throwing games or ticket sales, but I suppose none of those things were here when the Indians were. The Dutch called it Rabbit Island, but for that I see even less proof. The only rabbit within sight is the large pink one carried by a proud young girl across the street. The air is gently humid, as if tiny drops of water filled the space around me, and I realize that is exactly what humidity is, tiny drops of water.

A man sits down next to me on the bench. Cars drive past and two police officers walk by slowly, simultaneously eyeing nothing and everything. I check the time on my phone; she should be here any minute now. What will I say? How will I say it? I don't want to scare her away. I close my eyes and decide not to open them until I feel her presence. The scent from the ocean steps to the front of the line as soon as I shut one sense off, salty and heavy with molten seaweed. A lonely gull shrieks somewhere above– at least I only hear the one. Then, as if urged on by the gull, as if the gull was the trumpet announcing my arrival, a man's voice hesitantly penetrates the sheet of humidity. "John David?" Could it be an old friend, or a relative? But all the way out here, I can't believe it. I keep my eyelids clamped shut and concentrate on the voice. It has suddenly become very important to me to open them only when I feel her inhabit my space. It will be the ultimate proof that there really is a connection between us. "I can't open my eyes right now," I say into empty space. There's a sad sort of acceptance in the man's voice. "Oh, okay." But then he finds the courage to go on, he picks himself up and sputters out the words before he changes his mind. "I know this probably isn't what you expected, and I'm sorry that I led you on." He makes no sense whatsoever. Why must I always be accosted by ranting imbeciles when I just want to be left alone. Perhaps it's just like with dogs, they can sense if you're afraid of them, or if you want to pet them. I concentrate harder on feeling Diane's energy field, but the voice won't give me a break. "It's just that once I had started I couldn't go back. You know what I mean? You take one step and then it's too late to go back." I am struggling to feel anything as the man yaps about his problems and I decide to be rude. "I am actually waiting for someone, so if you'll excuse me." But half-wit just won't take a hint and continues blabbering. "Yeah, I know."

Somehow these words strike a chord in me, and I can't help but play along. "You do?" I say, thinking that perhaps Diane sent her friend over to check me out. And no matter how hard I concentrate, the voice shatters my world with one blow. "Because I am Diane," he says.

Allan and I ride the Ferris wheel. I am deeply disappointed, almost in shock. Allan is Diane. Diane is a man. Online Dating 101: never assume identity before it's confirmed. This is how bad men chat up underage girls, pretending to be someone else entirely. I feel like Dolly, seven years old, on a date with Allan (or, as his nick would have him called, "Tinderblossom") except that Allan isn't here to take advantage of me. In fact, Allan is very sorry for what he's done. He explains it to me, over and over again, with an earnest look plastered across his face, that he is truly sorry for not disclosing his true identity. It's just that, well, he doesn't have many friends. They don't come to him easily, either where he sits in his office prism, or in his home prism, and between the two he doesn't get out much. In short, Allan is even lonelier than me. So how can I really be upset with him? Me, the one who stalks pretty girls just so that I can imagine that we have a life together, if only for a few delusional blocks. I, who can't quite let go of the ex who has long since let go, moved on and maybe even forgot. I, who scour each online corner for dates to fill the void, hoping to find the perfect one. I am just like Allan, we are the same but for a few physical differences. Allan is balding, for one, and he is slightly overweight – the result of too many TV meals. Allan is partly a child in a man's body, but the man is there, I can tell, along with the child, both of whom desperately try to claw their way to some sort of identity. I know because I have this child inside who refuses to let go, refuses because he is afraid, and when the dark, threatening clouds congregate above he runs and hides in a closet that houses a fantasyland.

The Ferris wheel creaks and vibrates as it takes us on a dubious ride towards the top. It's a geriatric's final walk. I'm sure, one of these days, it will simply crumble to pieces. If that day is today, taking both me and Allan with it, that would be poetry in motion. The wheel stops moving when we are at the very top. We swing back and forth for a pending second or two, then the cart slides along the rails that run in an upside down s-shape and the cart moves down a notch and swings heavily back and forth. Neither Allan nor I grabs onto the bars. A seagull, perhaps the same gull I heard on the bench, flies by just out of reach. I'm pretty sure Allan is thinking what I am, that if we jumped from here we wouldn't have to deal with anything anymore. No more jobs we don't like, no more bills, no more trying, longing for the women we don't even know exist, attempting to climb out from the abyss of loneliness in which we somehow find ourselves. It would be a free fall of a few seconds, one, two, three, then it would be over. Who in their right mind wouldn't trade the world's hardship for eternal peace, when the price is only three seconds of terror? It's hard to believe that more people don't kill themselves. There's a reason to do it every day, there's disappointment on every corner, in every cereal box. "I'm not mad at you, Allan," I say. I feel at ease, sitting with him here in the gently rocking cart on top of the Ferris wheel, contemplating throwing myself info the lion's den below.

It's funny because despite it all, I feel we are true friends. Diane, Allan, they are but names and images in my imagination. Our conversations were real, our link-leaping, the humor that took us through the days, it was all real. "I'm just so lonely." I say it out loud. It's no mistake and it's not intentional, I just don't care anymore. I feel Allan's hand grab mine. It's soft as a baby's foot, and he squeezes it twice, as if to say, I hear you, it's going to be all right. Right then the Ferris wheel starts moving with a sour jerk. I squeeze Allan's hand back, silently thanking him, and that's that. We sit together in the rocking cart, going round and round, the entire universe over our heads and Coney Island with the ocean and the boardwalk and the old rides coming and going with each lap, and I no longer feel like killing myself. This is why, I realize, people don't do it on every street corner. The peculiar beauty of the world, the way it shines through when you least expect it. The touch of a stranger, the warming gesture of a friend, the way a seagull floats on the soft evening air, the beauty of loneliness. "Each coin has two sides," Allan says, as if to nail down what we feel deep in our souls, a life lesson that started a long time ago. Finally the Ferris wheel slows down and comes to a standstill with our cart level to the ground. The old man by the controls nods at us, as if he knew we had things to sort out and that the Ferris wheel was the place to do it, and he'd be damned if he was going to let us off before we were done and the experienced old machine had enlightened us.

Allan and I walk towards the exit. We stand right outside, opposite the bench we sat on only a short while ago, although it seems it was another life, another planet altogether. My fever is gone, everything is clearer, I'm no longer heavy laden with lead. "What now?" I say and look at Allan. He looks at me, sad at first, but that is only before his face cracks up with a smile. "We go on," he says, like some frontier man determined to find his destiny among the rolling hills in the distance. "Thanks, Allan," I say, and I give him a hug. It feels only natural. If not blood brothers, we are the next closest kind. "Ahhhh!" I scream, letting out a cubic foot of pent-up steam. I jump up and down on the sidewalk, shadow box, and scream "Ahhhh!" just because it feels good to be alive. "That's my ride,"

Allan says and waves a car in to the curb. He moves into the street, towards the passenger door, and when he does, revealed behind his body through the open side window, I spot a woman. There is something about her, something that no words dare even attempt to describe. She is not a redhead, more of a brunette, her eyes are large and don't really match her lips, and her entire face is sort of unproportional. She is simply indescribable, but she catches my eye and I can't stop looking. "This is my sister," Allan says. I just stare, unable to move. I've just landed from a vertical jump, my hands are halfway drawn up in a shadow-boxing position, and I just stand there looking the fool, unable to speak. "Hi," the woman says, and her voice, well, although indescribable, it is the voice I've always been looking for, pearly and seductive, like a stalling motor vehicle, and it purrs, "Nice to meet you," and she puts her hand through the open window. I still can't move, and in the periphery I see Allan bend over and whisper something in her ear. The woman opens her eyes a second time, although they are already open, and her lips mouths the words I thought were forever lost. "My name is Diane." Still unable to move, I am joyous on the inside, exuberant: fireworks go off all throughout my body, and I see all the beauty in the world at the same time. Life is coming full circle. Life is happening right now. Coney Island *is* J. D. Salinger. J. D. Salinger *is* Coney Island! What a world it is, what a wonderful, beautiful world it is.

THE END